Milson Alan is an educationalist with thirty-five years of experience. This is his first foray into the world of authorship. He always wanted to be a professional footballer but had to settle for being reasonably good at many sports. He is married and has three children. He enjoys playing the piano, singing in a choir, and is a keen swimmer. He travels to some quite interesting places!

I would like to dedicate this novel to British and American Special Forces who have worked, and still work behind enemy lines, in the shadows and the silence!

Whilst reading *To The Last Round* by Andrew Salmon, I came across a mention of two British soldiers who had been seconded to the American Special Services during the Korean War. Leo Adams-Acton and David Sharp. Whilst it was only a brief passage about them, it was the catalyst that I was looking for. Bravery and daring unheralded. Adams was killed at the age of 23 trying to escape from a prisoner of war camp after having shown extraordinary feats of courage in previous encounters with the enemy. David Sharp had the distinction of being the last POW to leave Chinese captivity.

To Kerry, my eldest daughter, for making me consider a more descriptive narrative with her questioning; reading my first draft, and making constructive suggestions. I only wrote it because you challenged me to write a book!

To Denise, my wife of 48 years, for her patience and constant encouragement.

To Penny and Alan Davies for reading my manuscript and believing that the story should be given to the world.

To Paul Davies who read my book on holiday and made such complimentary remarks.

To Lofty Wiseman, for being such a gentleman and being willing to swap stories and give advice about publishing in general. An honour to spend time with the great man,

I do not think I would have kept on sending my manuscript to publishers without your support.

Milson Alan

# THE RELUCTANT HERO

AUSTIN MACAULEY PUBLISHERS
LONDON · CAMBRIDGE · NEW YORK · SHARJAH

Copyright © Milson Alan 2025

The right of Milson Alan to be identified as author of this work has been asserted by the author in accordance with sections 77 and 78 of the Copyright, Designs and Patents Act 1988.

All rights reserved. No part of this publication may be reproduced, stored in a retrieval system, or transmitted in any form or by any means, electronic, mechanical, photocopying, recording, or otherwise, without the prior permission of the publishers.

Any person who commits any unauthorised act in relation to this publication may be liable to criminal prosecution and civil claims for damages.

This is a work of fiction. Names, characters, businesses, places, events, locales, and incidents are either the products of the author's imagination or used in a fictitious manner. Any resemblance to actual persons, living or dead, or actual events is purely coincidental.

A CIP catalogue record for this title is available from the British Library.

ISBN 9781035895755 (Paperback)
ISBN 9781035895762 (ePub e-book)

www.austinmacauley.com

First Published 2025
Austin Macauley Publishers Ltd®
1 Canada Square
Canary Wharf
London
E14 5AA

I would like to thank Katie Lewis from Austin Macauley for being very patient with all my initial questions. She allayed my fears!

# Table of Contents

| | |
|---|---|
| **Chapter 1: The Funeral** | 11 |
| **Chapter 2: And so it Begins** | 31 |
| **Chapter 3: The Black Book** | 40 |
| **Chapter 4: The Attack** | 63 |
| *This is What I Found Out About the Korean War* | 70 |
| **Chapter 5: Home Truths** | 86 |
| **Chapter 6: Kwanumsa Temple** | 96 |
| **Chapter 7: Adrift in a Sea of Uncertainty** | 111 |
| **Chapter 8: Bad News** | 126 |
| **Chapter 9: New Beginnings** | 142 |
| **Chapter 10: Saturday Night's Alright for Fighting** | 162 |
| **Chapter 11: Visitors** | 171 |
| **Chapter 12: A Nightmare of the Past** | 191 |
| **Chapter 13: In Memoriam** | 199 |
| **Chapter 14: Epilogue** | 216 |

# Chapter 1
# The Funeral

As a teenager, I haven't been to too many funerals, thankfully! The one I'm about to describe has the potential to be turned into a comedy-drama; with the right script writer/director/producer, it would be an award-winner, a best-seller and a blockbusting cinematic delight!

Oh, by the way, my name is Kerry Morgan. I'm 18 years old, a girl with dark brown hair and eyes and am quite tall being 5ft 10 inches. I'm sat in a chapel. A Welsh Baptist Chapel to be accurate, in deepest, darkest West Wales. It is 15 March 2018 and it is a wet, cold day; not unusual for the time of year. The service is all in Welsh and it is my grandfather's funeral; he died of a heart attack at the age of 93. His name was Johnny Morgan: he did not speak Welsh, attend the chapel, or agree to be buried, but wanted to be cremated; but my nan decided otherwise. Well, he couldn't complain from beyond the grave—could he?

Our family group is seated in the central section of pews; in the front two rows uncomfortably near the preacher and the pulpit. The chapel is austere with shiny honey-coloured brown wood a dominant feature of the heavily varnished, stick-to-your-bottom type. The gloomy morning light lances through the unadorned glass windows giving the effect of searchlights seeking out a target. The floor is carpeted throughout in a dusky cerise colour with geometrical shapes of blues and blacks overlaid. The pulpit itself is reached by two access points symmetrically placed; the climb being up four carpeted steps. Then there is a balustrade of the same wood with turned spindles and posts grinning down at us like a gap-toothed giant. There is a lectern centrally placed at which the minister peers down at his congregation dispensing the word of God.

Mr Thewlis, the preacher, is dressed in a sombre black, well-cut suit. He is short in stature but broad in chest. He is clean-shaven and has an interesting bowling ball head sat on a very thick heavily veined neck leading down to immense shoulders and well-developed, muscular arms. His suit jacket strains to keep his torso in. He speaks through the side of his mouth in a high-pitched squeaky soprano voice. The congregation don't seem to find his voice amusing. Perhaps they have got used to its timbre. But I feel like hooting with laughter and glancing at my brother and sister I can see that their shoulders are synchronised in barely noticeable up and down movements suggesting that they are having difficulty keeping their mirth contained inside their bodies.

Behind Mr Thewlis is a large piped organ with highly decorated tubes diving down to the double keyboard with creamy-looking organ stops on either side; at which sits a very ancient, gnarled, rheumy-eyed, suited and booted gentleman organist. He is alert; with furtive movements of his head constantly viewing the two mirrors that enable him to see the audience and whoever is standing at the lectern. It appears as if he is judging the use of wing mirrors in a vehicle to decide to reverse into a rather narrow parking space. I can see his face reflected in the left mirror and he seems to have a rather nasty twitch in his left eye that suggests that he is winking all the time. The organ pipes are easily the most ornate part of the chapel in an otherwise 'Spartan' place of worship. There is an upper floor with further tiered seating where my dad used to sit when he was a boy. Boredom apparently allowed his imagination to run wild and he often day-dreamed that the chapel had been converted into—wait for it—yes an indoor swimming pool!

The downstairs would be filled up to the bottom of the upstairs balustrade with salt water. He imagined there was an array of diving boards off the upper floor and whatever minister was preaching at the time was dressed in a lifeguard's costume. The minister would have to dive elegantly into the pool; the congregation would then score the effort out of ten and the overall score would be put up on the thickly lacquered shiny brown hymn board and then everyone would sing that number song found in the hymn book. He did say that his imagination was so good that he could still remember the smell of the salt and the unpleasant body and foot odours. He even had an out-of-body experience during sermons of the direst length when he was manoeuvring underwater between the pews and having to come up for breath before diving again to explore dark nooks and crannies. Moray eels and exotic fish were all chased during these descents into vividly waking dreams.

I suppose attending chapel three times on a Sunday and once on a Wednesday for a 'band of hope' (whatever that is) can do that to an impressionable young mind. But I do think my dad has a screw loose and my mum definitely thinks so!

My dad's name is Alan Morgan and my mum is Denise. Going back to the Welsh; it is not just in Welsh, it is highbrow bible-Welsh. Even my grandmother who is a regular chapel-goer and a fluent Welsh speaker can't understand a great deal of what the preacher Mr Thewlis is on about as he tends to spout in very archaic Welsh. As the service progresses, a male voice choir powerfully leads the singing: then readings, hymns, more hymns, and a medley of songs by the choir that Granddad was a member of. My mind wanders, interrupted by my grandmother constantly shouting, 'Ie' which in English means 'Yes' whilst Mr Thewlis is speaking. A number of local people who were obviously friends, stand at the lectern and espouse how great a man my granddad was. It seems strange to me as I've never seen or heard of these people and they seem to speak as if they knew him well.

I was born in the city of Hereford as were my siblings. Dad has a job there that takes him away from us for long periods of time. All he does say is that he works for the 'Foreign Office', whatever that means, and that he met Mum in Hereford. My dad, who is sitting next to me, is a proud Welshman; you know—rugby, singing and religion—although the religion bit has lapsed considerably.

I glance around at the congregation and it is well worth the movement. I scan inquisitively, noticing the male voice choir that my granddad sang in for nearly fifty years situated en-masse in the centre on the two back row pews; attired in leaf green, badged blazers, dark trousers and white shirts with green ties. At quiet moments during proceedings, the careful unwrapping of boiled sweets can just about be heard emanating from this group and there is a wafting smell of 'fisherman's friends' lozenges in the air. Oiling their voices never appeared or sounded so sweet! I remembered that Granddad always had a peppermint scent whenever he had been to choir practise. Small groups of older ladies dressed in black with heavily creased faces are dotted around the space; the heavy mingling of different perfumes tickling the olfactory glands almost to the level of sneezing, but not quite! Obviously, friends of Nan, lend their support at a difficult time! Going back to Dad's imagined vision of the inside of the chapel being a swimming pool; at least now there wasn't the smell of brine coupled with the pong of sweaty feet! He has obviously pulled me into his delusional behaviour. A smattering of grey-haired old men were distributed in pairs with heads bowed, trying to remain unnoticed; whilst in another section, a much larger group of men, who exuded what can only be described as 'military bearing'. You know, short hair, erect postures, black great coats and alert group coordinated movements.

Interestingly, there is also a very well-dressed woman, wearing an expensive-looking hat which hangs at a jaunty angle; pierced by a single grey feather. She looks in her seventies. She is sat near the military-bearing group; she is accompanied by two very fit, but fierce-looking young men in well-cut suits. Perhaps, they are her sons, but I doubted it, as they seemed too alert in the confines of the Chapel. I would like to know what had brought them to the funeral service.

Towards the end of the service, Mr Thewlis, asked in English, if anyone else in the congregation would like to say anything further about the deceased.

Two men rise from the 'military-bearing group' and head towards the pulpit. I sit up at this point and I think most of my family do as well. The lead gentleman is tall and very broad-shouldered. He removes a black full-length coat and lays it carefully on a chair nearby. The removal of the coat reveals that he is wearing a military uniform—it is a green colour with lots of polished silver buttons and on his left side is an array of medals. He wears a leather belt around his waist that then loops away over a shoulder.

The gentleman cleared his throat and began to speak:

*I am here to represent the thoughts of my fellow 'band of military brothers' who all knew Johnny. I first met Johnny Morgan during the latter stages of the Second World War and then latterly whilst we were both serving in the Korean War. Throughout our military time together he was conscientious, thoroughly committed to the cause, highly intelligent and though rather quiet had a well-developed sense of humour. He was a brave, courageous man who had a high regard for fair play and was a good comrade to many of us. It is right to say that some of us would not be here today if it were not for his bravery in extreme circumstances.*

*Sadly, his own country has not fully managed to acknowledge his courageous deeds. We are here today because we wanted people to know that he was a hero to us and many others! He was someone we all aspired to be! My colleagues in the audience and I were members of the Korean War Veterans Association until it was discontinued a few years ago. We as a group felt it was important to keep up the memory of that terrible war by still supporting members and their families in any way we could. We are here today because Johnny was one of us. In fact, for most of us, he was our hero!*

*I amongst others have been putting pressure on the British government to recognise more fully what Johnny did during the Korean War and I can tell you that support is beginning to gain momentum in military circles. I cannot say too much more, but watch this space!*

With that, the gentleman stepped back from the lectern and stood at attention with his head bowed!

I didn't even know he had been in the army. My parents or grandparents had not mentioned that Granddad Johnny had a military past!

When the next man moved to the lectern, I sat up even further in my seat as when he removed his topcoat, he revealed a dark blue uniform with very ornate trimmings of gold and also a colourful, plentiful row of medals. He was quite short in stature for a soldier and he spoke with an American accent and had a very swarthy, almost Asian complexion.

*I also met Johnny when in Korea. I was just eighteen. He rescued me and many others from a prisoner-of-war camp well behind enemy lines and with partisan fighters led us to safety through those enemy lines. The conditions in the camp were brutal and many of us had given up hope of survival so when Johnny and his team rescued us the light came back into our eyes.*

*When we thanked him, he was extremely modest and reserved, saying he was just doing his duty. You should all feel very proud of having met and spent time with this man. He was very proud of being Welsh, even though we all thought he was English. He said that he came from the land of the red dragon and ended up a white tiger, which was the name of the group he worked for in Korea. He was an exceptional human being; kind and courageous but also humble. The world is a lesser place for his passing. I don't know if Mildred recognises me or remembers me, but I was Johnny's best man at their wedding. That was fifty-four years ago, believe it or not.*

This man spoke with an American accent tinged with a Spanish lilt and I sensed from the way his voice crackled with emotion that he had a strong affection and respect for Granddad Johnny. His eulogy brought a lump to my throat and tears to my eyes. He must have been some sort of man that these people would travel such long distances after so many years to remember him. After the second gentleman spoke, they both left the platform.

When the two military gentlemen had returned to their seats, there was an interminable silence until a lone hand slowly rose and the owner of the hand asked if he could say a few words. Mr Thewlis beckoned the man forward. The congregation as one followed, almost robotically, the man from his place.

I peered between the heads and shoulders of people and saw that he was in his seventies; he walked in an upright, assured manner. His shoes squeaked loudly on the rich, dusky cerise carpet as each stride took him closer to the steps up to the pulpit. It was as if the audience had all taken a deep breath at the same time and were holding it to see how long they could last. The man had a full head of dark brown hair, streaked with a few strands of salt and pepper touches. He had very alert, sparkling green eyes that suggested a mischievous nature. He climbed fluidly up to the lectern and in that moment I noticed a dimpled chin. I smiled to myself and quietly noted that he had to be related to Granddad Johnny, although I had never seen him before. I turned my head to Dad and whispered, "Now who can this be?"

Dad nodded in the negative suggesting he didn't know either. At that moment, the congregation exhaled in unison with a whooshing sigh and seemed to shift noticeably forward in their seats. The gentleman cleared his throat and here is what he said:

*I almost talked myself out of speaking, after listening to you all say such lovely things about Johnny. As this is a time to record aspects of his life I couldn't let the opportunity pass, as I believe I'm the only one here to have known him a lifetime. My name is Philip Morgan. Johnny was my big brother!*

He paused and so did the audience. Even my nan looked up at the pulpit in astonishment! The stunned silence was back. I glanced back at the sea of concentrating, creased faces, which it seemed, had moved en-masse even further forward. I could see that my nan's two sisters had the cogs of curiosity whirring inside their puzzled heads. Even in three sentences, you could tell that he was either American or Canadian. From the look on people's faces, no one knew of this man. He gave a slight cough and began again.

*Johnny was fifteen years older than me. I was only two when he left to join the army at the age of seventeen. He wasn't supposed to join the army but a family tragedy led him down that path. You see, my mother was killed by my father. Dad had a piece of shrapnel in his skull from the First World*

*War which they couldn't remove and it affected him mentally. He would have hallucinations and memory lapses. My brothers and sisters told me that he had always been a happy and kind person who would not hurt a soul.*

*However, his behaviour, because of the war wound, became more and more erratic and violent, culminating in the insane act. Johnny was present at the time and tried to intervene. He was seriously injured and it took six months for him to recover from the brutal injuries he sustained. We lost two parents on that fateful day. Dad was placed in a sanatorium for the insane and died there. Before his death, I believe that Johnny visited him, whenever he was home from the army. When Johnny recovered from the terrible assault, he told my other brother Ed that he would never be in a situation again where he couldn't protect the people he loved and the next day enlisted in the army.*

*My sister Glenys was brave enough, at the age of 23, to adopt me. However, after the Second World War, we immigrated to Canada. I was just six years old. Her husband, Ronnie, was a mining engineer and worked in the mining areas of the Yukon Territory. Johnny came to visit us in 1950 when I was 10 years old. This was before he went to Korea. I remember playing football with him and going on long walks. We both enjoyed the outdoors. He was a quiet man who tended to keep his thoughts to himself. He never ever spoke about what had happened to Mum and Dad. He came to visit us again when I reached the age of 13. He was even less talkative by then. We could all see that the Korean War had left him exhausted physically and mentally. He stayed with us for around six weeks.*

*Fortunately, it was the summer vacation and we spent our time kayaking, sailing, swimming and rock-climbing. Whilst he didn't talk a lot he was good fun to be with and I absolutely idolised him. I saw him again in 1958 when I turned 18. He stayed for a month and we had such a great time. The last time I actually saw Johnny was in 1970. Anyway, I'm rambling and that wasn't my intention. I'm the only one left now so when a friend of mine told me that Johnny had died I had to be here. I loved and admired him. I am proud to have called him brother.*

With that, Philip Morgan left the pulpit, all eyes followed him as he walked down the aisle; but instead of going back to his seat, he left the building quietly, leaving everyone wondering if we had all been in a collective dream delivered by an apparition. I think everyone in the congregation was stunned and saddened by what he had said. There was an awkward silence that had dampened the atmosphere, yes even of a funeral!

Just as the minister was about to announce the last hymn I stood up and quietly said, "I'd like to speak about Granddad Johnny if you don't mind, Mr Thewlis." My entire family looked surprised at my sudden request. It was a spur-of-the-moment decision on my part, I suppose, in an attempt to raise the mood of everyone in the congregation. The minister nodded in an understanding way and before I knew it I was standing nervously holding the lectern and looking down at the congregation. What could I say? The silence was palpable as I fidgeted at the lectern. My legs were like quivering sticks of celery, but then it all came flowing out:

*I've only known my granddad a short while compared to many of you so my thoughts are probably not as deep and meaningful. However, from the time I was old enough to be aware of him, I always felt safe in his company. He was a clever man with a well-developed, quirky sense of humour. He seemed to have a knack with engines and could sort out most mechanical problems. The stories that he told us kids suggested his family did not have a lot of money but they were nevertheless happy with their lives and made the most of things. He was quite a mischief-maker when he was a boy and the stories he used to tell about tricks they played around the outside toilet are notoriously disgusting and perhaps not for the telling here. We used to play card games with him and he was such a big cheat. He would hide cards up his sleeve, under his leg, anywhere and then divert our attention away from the cheating.*

*My nan always told us to watch him but we didn't catch him until we were much older. I think he must have taught my dad those tricks as well. Daaad! He could tell a good story and loved his wife, grandkids and his own kids dearly. I know he would do anything for us, even give his life I'm sure! I didn't know he was in the army but I'm quite sure he would have been really good at it as he had the ability and focus to be good at anything he put his mind to. A funny story springs to mind about Granddad Johnny which I'd like to share with you. My brother, sister and I spent the afternoon with Granddad when we were still in primary school and the four of us went into Nan's best room and for some strange reason, we started throwing around my brother's soft toy. It was an ant eater called Andy. As we tossed the toy creature around,*

Granddad started singing a song from a First War medley that he sang with his choir. It went like this:

Over there, over there, send the word, send the word, over there...and here's the funny part...That the Ants are coming, the Ants are coming—instead of—the Yanks are coming. We laughed and laughed because, of course, Andy the anteater would love that song. I suppose you had to be there to appreciate the cleverness but whenever we were with Granddad after that, we would remind him by singing the song to him. I'm sure the choir will appreciate the humour. Well, to finish the story Nan has some rather nice porcelain King Charles dogs on the mantlepiece in the best room and one of Granddad's throws went wrong and guess what happened...yes, the soft toy knocked one of the dogs off the mantlepiece. It landed on the hard, tiled surface below and some pieces were knocked off the dog. Well, we were all in a panic.

Nan would be absolutely furious on three counts. Firstly, we had gone into the front room; secondly, we had been playing catch in her best room and thirdly we had smashed a prized ornament. Granddad told us all to calm down. He went out into the garage and came back with some ceramic glue and we all collected the pieces together and then proceeded to attempt a repair. Fortunately, the damage had been done to the back of the porcelain dog. After we had glued all the pieces, Granddad picked the dog up and put it back on the mantlepiece. He laughed and said, "There, she'll never know. She never comes in here anyway." I'm not sure Nan ever found out but I'm sure I'll find out later on today. Finally, I would like to say that if I grow up to be a fraction of the person

*Granddad Johnny was I will be a happy and lucky person and at this point, I better sit down before I blubber my heart out!*

With that, I swiftly left the lectern, hot tears streaming down my face, my eyes fixed only on my place in the second row, knowing that if I looked towards anyone now I would crumble completely. I only hoped that my account had lifted the spirits of the congregation a little. My dad gave me a nudge and said, "That was clever and brave of you!" I sat in my own little world for a moment until I looked towards my family. They all gave sad smiles.

My nan turned to me and said, "Da iawn ti," which means 'very good you'. The last hymn was: 'Hen wlad fy nhadau' which is the Welsh National Anthem—translated it means 'Old Land of my Fathers'. After the singing, the preacher invited the whole congregation to attend my nan's house for food and hot drinks. My dad whispered under his breath, "There won't be any alcohol, as they are teetotal. I could do with a stiff drink."

After the chapel service ended the oak coffin of lightly coloured brown was carried back to the jet-black hearse by the six pallbearers. They slid the coffin onto some rollers and my dad Alan, his two brothers and three cousins stepped back respectfully whilst the undertakers took over by placing wreaths and bouquets of flowers on the coffin lid before carefully closing the hearse's boot. The pallbearers joined us on the route up the path to the cemetery; the cold morning air collided with people's exhaling breath creating wispy tendrils of whiteness, dissipating quickly in the gentle breeze. The gradient was too steep and the graveside too far for the pallbearers to manage the coffin comfortably so the coffin was transported by car to an entrance closer to the graveyard.

I kept an eye out for Philip Morgan but he was nowhere to be seen. As I've already observed many of the congregation were elderly so there were numerous stops for gulps of air making the trek laborious up the footpath leading to the cemetery perched precariously on the hillside. Gun metal grey clouds clung heavily to the meandering slope giving a feeling of moving through smoke with the outline of the mourners and the myriad of gravestones blurring in the ethereal light. We eventually arrived at the plot and the second part of the service began. No sooner had the coffin been lowered into the ground than my nan tried to jump in on top of the coffin.

Well, it started off more like a dance around the edge of the hole and as she is not exactly a prima ballerina the whole episode looked hilarious. Luckily, a sympathetic soul grabbed her before she managed to dive in and hugged her close. I noticed that the elderly lady who had been accompanied in the chapel by the two young men remained towards the back of the group of mourners. Where were the young men? I looked around casually and noticed that they had taken up separate positions a little way from the mourners and were glancing around in a state of great alertness. How curious!

The service at the graveside ended with people dropping soil into the hole with some white roses, lilies and other flowers following. The roses and lilies gave off a refreshing fragrance accentuated by the cold, biting air. Before we left the graveside a phalanx of smartly dressed, rifle-armed, soldiers approached. They were dressed in green uniforms and had sandy-coloured berets on which flying dagger insignias were pinned centrally. The medals on the left side of their chests sparkled in the morning light. I couldn't help but notice how shiny their black shoes were. They came to a halt quite near the mourners. A bugler stood to one side and played 'The Last Post', each note echoing sombrely over the hillside. They formed a line and were called to attention by an officer who then shouted 'Present arms and…fire!' The sound of gunfire on the previously silent hillside was thunderous in its volume and shocking in its way. The reverberations bounced off the surrounding gravestones and continued the sound for seconds after. My nan wailed bitterly the whole time.

My nan's name is Mildred Arianwen Morgan but her sons call her 'Mam', her grandchildren—Nan, and anyone else who knows her as Mil.

With the service concluded, there was a mad scramble to get off the cold hillside. Warmth was needed and sustenance was waiting. Although for many of the congregation that meant gingerly, careful and slow withdrawals down the slope.

My dad stayed at the graveside after everyone else had gone so our little family made up of me, Mum, younger brother Liam and younger sister Rhianna stayed with him. He thanked the soldiers for the military honour of a gun salute and then wandered among the gravestones visiting my Great-Nan's grave and his friend John's grave. I followed him, whilst the others just wandered aimlessly, occasionally stopping to read what it said on a gravestone.

One of the more senior-looking soldiers followed Dad. I heard him say, "Johnny used to come up to Hereford and instruct us on unarmed combat techniques. He must have been in his seventies by then but no one messed with him. I saw him demonstrate how to go about fighting three opponents and he put them down without breaking into a sweat." Dad thanked the officer for sharing his thoughts about Granddad Johnny and then continued to speak to the two headstones he had come to visit. He kept on saying that they must all appreciate the grand view over the Loughor estuary away to the Gower Peninsula.

I groaned and rolled my eyes before saying, "But they are all dead so it doesn't matter to them!"

He winked and replied, "Yeah, but their spirits might like the view!" I asked Dad about how come the soldiers were there and all he could say was that the men who spoke must have arranged it. Whilst we all headed back to the car to go to Nan's house for some food and a cup of tea, I asked my dad what it was like carrying the coffin and he said thoughtfully, "Well, it felt a lot heavier when we had to carry him back to the hearse after the chapel service and he seemed to move around in the box more."

I said, "I'm not surprised considering he didn't want to be buried in the first place!"

Then out of the corner of my eye, I could see someone approaching Granddad Johnny's grave. It was Philip. He stood with his head bowed and was sobbing quietly to himself. I touched Dad on the shoulder and said, "Look!"

"Yes, I know he's there," Dad stated quietly. "Let's give him some space, eh! I'll stick around and talk to him if you lot head to the 'wake' with your mum."

The wake was very interesting from the perspective of an eighteen-year-old. Neighbours provided the food— sandwiches, cakes, quiches, sausage rolls, cheese and pineapple on a stick whilst the hostess provided the plates and drinks. I tried to help as best I could but in the end, decided to mingle with the mourners. Some of the old ladies, who were obviously dressed in their Sunday best and had visited the hairdressers for blue and pink rinses, were in competition with each other over who provided the best cakes or savouries. I was given a slice of Victoria sandwich cake, with raspberry jam oozing out of the sides, and no sooner had I taken a bite than another old lady came up and said, "You won't enjoy that dear, try this," and scooped the original off my plate. The competition I think was at its most fierce with the quiches. I was given a slice of cheese and bacon quiche and whilst appreciating my first bite was confronted by a lady of mature years saying, "It's got a 'soggy bottom', hasn't it, dear?"

I tried to mumble between mouthfuls, "No it hasn't. It's delicious!"

Before I had said, "No," the piece was spirited away replaced by her own effort, which quite honestly was inferior. I felt like approaching Nan and telling her about what was going on but thought better of it considering what her mind must be going through trying to process the reality and finality of what was happening. I did hope that the mysterious elderly lady and the two handsome young men had come to have some food but was disappointed.

I had tried hard to stay away from my nan as she was emotionally unhinged, talking to herself and sobbing uncontrollably at different times. Obviously, it was not surprising considering that they had been married for over fifty-four years so I became quite nervous when she came to sit next to me and said, "Your granddad Johnny liked your inquisitive and curious nature, 'bach' and wanted me to give you this letter from him after the funeral so there I've done it. Oh and yes, I did know about the King Charles Spaniel! I thought it was quite funny!" and with that, she drifted off to speak to one of her sisters; I think it was Eleri.

I held the cream envelope delicately in my hands, wondering where I could discretely place it about my person. I am quite resistant to carrying handbags so was about to ask my dad to carry it for me in his jacket pocket when my nan's other sister Eilwen flopped heavily into the seat next to me. Eilwen is a retired school teacher and the twin sister of Eleri, although you wouldn't know it to look at them. Eleri has the stature of a small bird whilst Eilwen is a more robust intimidating figure. Think Miss Trunchbull!

Being a teacher, she had the ability to make you feel guilty even though you hadn't done anything wrong and I felt under close scrutiny as she stared expectantly at me. "Aren't you going to open it then?" She quizzed.

"Open what?" I replied cautiously.

"The envelope Johnny left for you, of course," she retorted leaning forward curiously.

"Well, I don't think now is the right time to start reading, it seems so rude in front of all these people," I replied respectfully.

Eilwen looked disappointed but accepted my reasoning and then said, "I better see if Mr Thewlis wants another salmon and cucumber sandwich," and with that, creaked to her feet and wobbled uncertainly away. I sat back and listened to the chatter all around me. I heard an old gentleman say to another much younger man, 'This is Mil's son Alan' and my dad joined them to have a conversation about the trials and tribulations of the Welsh rugby team. It struck me that Milson Alan would be a brilliant name for an actor or a novelist. I asked him about Philip Morgan and all Dad could quietly say was, "He gave me a lift here and was going to come in but I think the raw emotion he was feeling prevented him. He's given me the name of the hotel he's staying in and his mobile number so I'll contact him later. I think he was going back to the graveside to quietly say his 'farewell'."

Oh my, it was certainly a tear-jerker of a day!

# Chapter 2
# And so it Begins

The letter was beginning to intrigue me so I went from the lounge into the front room. The Welsh call it the 'best room' and it is kept for special occasions with the best furniture, carpets and ornaments; but nobody is allowed in there. Clearly, my granddad's funeral did not warrant its use today. The contents of the room seemed to have been untouched for at least fifty years. A time capsule from the 1960s! There was a large proportioned three-piece suit in a pink colour with tassels touching the floor which overly dominated the room. The carpet had a deep pile and was luxurious to walk on. It almost felt sacrilegious to walk on it in outdoor footwear. It was a mixture of different red and pink hues. In front of the sofa was a round black and white tiled mosaic table with black wooden legs that looked as if it could do with a dusting. There was a white tiled fireplace and on the mantelpiece was a small carriage clock and positioned at either end two china King Charles dogs.

I walked over to the dog on the left-hand side of the mantlepiece and picked it up. I checked the back and smiled to myself. There were two display cabinets with an array of porcelain figures of ladies in beautiful, formal dresses. A pair of heavy powdery pink curtains framed the bay window creating the effect of formality. I sat in the middle of the sofa and to my surprise, the cushion beneath me was very firm suggesting that very few people had ever had the opportunity to sit down in that room. I opened the envelope and drew out the folded cream paper. There were only two mysterious sentences on the page.

The first sentence from my granddad asked me to go into the attic and retrieve a box which was situated to the right of the water tank. The letter also instructed me to do this without telling others what was in the box as I was the only one to know its secrets for the time being.

My nan had told me previously when she had asked me to fetch some Christmas decorations from the attic, that to get into the space, I needed to push the attic hatch with a pole situated beneath it. Once the hatch dropped down, there was a chain that could be pulled to lower down a metal staircase. This I did and when I reached the top step, I felt something drop into my hair and it made me shudder with disgust. I hate cobwebs and spiders. I climbed up into the attic. At that point, I dragged my long dark hair over my ears, pulled my fleece hood up and zipped my top up to under my chin; to protect myself from little hairy beasts!

My nan had told me that there was a light switch to the right of the hatch within touching distance. I felt around and heard the satisfying click of the switch accompanied by the faint reassuring glow of a light directly above. As I moved further into the attic space, I had to step along planks laid over beams heading towards the water tank. I saw in the gloomy light a small table and chair perched on a rectangular planked area in the attic; probably where Granddad would sit when he did some writing. I couldn't for the life of me understand why he had to write in secret. I know writing is a solitary business but to go into a cold attic space I just couldn't fathom.

Arrayed around the attic space were: a dusty mirror, an old rocking chair on which I had sat as a small child, and some Christmas paraphernalia that included: a plastic Christmas tree, a plastic lobster attached to a piece of wood; and one of those silly fish that wriggles and sings when you touch its tail. My grandparents must have been real 'suckers' for silly Christmas gadgets that sang Christmas tunes. I was tempted to press the buttons on the tree, lobster and fish to see which tunes would be played but I stopped myself just in time. After all, I was there to do a job! The box was found easily. The box felt heavily carved on the top and sides whilst very smooth on the base. It was a hefty weight with very little movement of its contents. I had to head back to the hatch with the box carried in both hands making it a bit of a balancing act. Switching the light off and turning to descend the metal ladder challenged my coordination skills but I managed it.

Back in the front room, I sat on the settee and had a cursory look at the box. It was ornate with carvings of red dragons and white tigers all over. I lifted the lid and peered curiously inside. I was expecting a musty smell considering where I had retrieved the box from! However, it was a pleasant pine fresh smell! The box was lined with green, silky fabric, on which were decorated white tigers and red dragons. On top of the contents was a sheet of cream paper from my granddad to me, written in a very neat cursive style whilst beneath was a rather thick black book. A quick glance through the pages revealed it to be written in Granddad Johnny's neat style, but what drew my attention were the other contents.

There were numerous medals, two berets of maroon and beige with cap badges of flying daggers; the same badges as the honour guard of soldiers were wearing at the graveside. There were some green stones and old black and white photographs of a young granddad Johnny in military uniform. The green stones were comma-shaped with one hole through the centre of each; there were 12 pieces in all. I went back to my granddad's letter and read:

*Dear Kerry,*

*If you are reading this, then I have obviously passed away. I've had a good and interesting life so do not feel too sad for me. In fact, knowing how curious you are, this may well prove to be an all-engrossing interest, with the possibility of putting your thoughts into some form of writing. I charge you with telling my story in all of its twists and turns. My diary covers my military history and personal life in the main, a great deal of it before I met your nan. You may be surprised by its contents. There are some sensitive issues within the pages of the black book that I think you should discuss with your dad before explaining to your nan. I don't want her feelings hurt but eventually, all my secrets will have to be told.*

*During the Korean War, I was seconded from the 21st Artists Rifles (S.A.S.) to the Glosters (The Gloucestershire Regiment) as their intelligence officer with the rank of 2nd Lieutenant. The eventual intention was for me to join up with partisans and US military advisers behind enemy lines to disrupt the effectiveness of the enemy. As I was separated from my regiment at the Imjin River, I ended up behind enemy lines before I was supposed to. By pure coincidence, I stumbled across the US special operations group that I had been assigned to join two months before the official time. Working with the partisans, who were anti-communists, our job was: to destroy and disrupt North Korean and Chinese supply lines; attack military and communication installations; rescue prisoners of war and downed aircraft personnel; collect intelligence about the distribution of troops; and call in air strikes on military targets. We were called the white tigers.*

*Now to tell you about the contents of the box:*

*There are twelve medals that have been awarded to me and they range from the Second World War to the Malayan Emergency. To be honest, they do not mean a lot to me. All I know is a lot of sadness is associated with them and for that reason, I have never worn them or shown them to anyone, not even your nan. I see men and women proudly wearing their medals on Remembrance Sunday but for some reason, I cannot show my medals to anyone. It's not that I'm ashamed of what I've done but I don't feel the need to highlight my military activities. My two SAS berets are very dear to me as whenever I put them on, they take me to vivid memories of the actions I was involved in and the people I served with at the time. There are five other medals which belonged to my father—William Morgan. He was with the South Wales Borderers in South Africa and the Welch regiment during the First World War. He was severely injured at a place called Mametz Wood during the First World War.*

*The green jewellery—first of all, they are worth a great deal of money—I really mean a lot of money, Kerry! In fact, be careful, as they are highly sought after by collectors. Please give them to your nan. They are called GOGOK. They are made from a precious stone called jadeite (not nephrite jade—this is an important point). Apparently, the stones were family heirlooms, passed down through the generations and are very old. I was given them by a wealthy Korean family for saving one of their children. Her name was Mi Yong. I later had a romance with the girl I saved and she became pregnant. I had to go to Tokyo to report to US special operations on the success of the partisans and whilst away the baby was born. Shortly after the birth and before I had returned to Korea, the girl I loved was captured and the partisan stronghold in the mountains was overrun and destroyed. She, amongst others, was executed by the North Korean army for being an insurgent. We intended to marry after the war had ended but unfortunately, fate took a different direction.*

*This is, even for me writing now, a heart-breaking episode in my life which I have never told your nan about or anyone else for that matter! A child being born out of wedlock in my day was frowned upon, to say the least, and I suppose that is perhaps the reason I have never told your nan. The people of Korea were even more traditional in their views and racial impurity, on top of being born out of wedlock, would have made the situation difficult. I was informed by a partisan who had escaped the attack, that my little baby girl, Mul Yong, which in our language translates as Water Dragon, was saved and was to be taken further north by her extended family the Yi clan. He told me that the baby had a white complexion, jet-black hair and astonishingly blue eyes, also, the very striking feature of a dimpled chin.*

*I have never seen or had contact with her. If she is still alive, then she would be sixty-six years of age. She may have children and even grandchildren. It has been my greatest regret that I have never been able to make contact with her.*

*The relationship North Korea has with the rest of the world has made it all but impossible for me to trace her whereabouts; although I have tried discretely so as not to draw attention from the authorities there considering I was helping the anti-communist partisans.*

Oh my goodness! My eyes prickled and I felt them well up with tears. I took a deep calming breath and put the letter down. A whirr of questions buzzed around in my head. My granddad must have been so sad and to tell anyone of this must have been heart-wrenching. I would have to tell Dad about this as it is too difficult to keep to oneself. I continued to read:

*Going back to the jadeite; the stones have rarely been seen over the sixty years I've had them. I must admit I have had to sell one or two. The black book is filled with memories but the writing is not in any particular order as I wrote when the need took me and my thoughts were written well after any incidents I describe so may well not be wholly accurate. It was a cathartic experience which helped me a great deal in reconciling what I did and what I could not do anything about. There may be some old comrades of mine attending the funeral and if you get the chance, introduce yourself and tell them that your granddad has given you the responsibility of telling his story and I'm sure they will be most cooperative and helpful.*

*There should be a Mexican/American amongst them by the name of Tom Bonilla—now his stories are really worth a listen! He is the salt of the earth and would do anything for me or anyone close to me. My brother Philip may also be in attendance. Yes, I know this revelation of me having a mysterious brother will come as a shock to you all but circumstances and geographical distance have played their roles in keeping us apart. I know the wake will be fairly full on so try to take contact details of some of these men so you can contact them at a later date. Good luck and you never know this may be the start of an exciting literary career.*

That must have been the second military man who had talked about Granddad at the funeral. So he was a Mexican/American. I've never met anyone before from Mexico so that should be an interesting experience. Well, Granddad's brother Philip certainly made himself known.

I was interrupted at this point by my nan shouting for me to come and help in the kitchen, so I put the letter back in the box and scanned the room for a safe hiding place. I settled on placing the box behind one of the powder pink curtains. As I lifted the curtain away, a cloud of dust made me cough and then sneeze. I closed the door quietly to the time capsule and rushed into the occupied rooms of the house.

The wake was coming to an end with people saying their farewells. I gave my biggest beaming smile as I approached the huddled group of old soldiers and found Tom Bonilla talking to the other gentleman who had spoken. I introduced myself and thanked them all for making such an effort to attend Granddad Johnny's funeral. I asked a number of them where they had travelled from. Harry Thomas, the first gentleman to have spoken surprised me by saying, "Cimla, near Neath." And when I asked Tom, he replied, "Mexico City." The others seemed to come from different parts of the UK and reaffirmed that they had been members of 'The Korean Veterans

Association' before it had been discontinued in 2014. They further explained that they continued to attend funerals as a group. I explained quietly to Tom Bonilla what my granddad had 'charged' me with doing. He smiled mischievously and stated that it was typical of my granddad to do things unconventionally. He said that he would help in any way he could and that I could rely on him to be the contact for access to the thoughts of other Korean veterans. He gave me his mobile number and his email address and then departed.

Before I knew it, we were clearing away and all the extended family were pitching in to wash up and tidy the place. Close family members said their goodbyes with lots of hugs and kisses and congratulated each other on how well everything had gone. There were lots of promises to meet up more often but geographical distance and just getting on with life always seems to prevent good intentions. We did not stay for very long afterwards. I managed to discretely retrieve the box from the front room and put it quietly in our car's boot.

My dad spent some time talking and reassuring my nan. We all climbed in the car feeling fairly emotionally drained by the day. Dad said that he just wanted to make a little detour into Llanelli to visit Philip. We sat in the car for about twenty minutes and he returned looking quite sad and forlorn. He explained that he had invited Philip Morgan to visit us the next day in an attempt to cheer the man up and perhaps get to know him a little better. We then headed back to our home which was a two-hour car journey away.

Fortunately, it was the beginning of the Easter holidays and I would have plenty of time to begin the journey of discovery my granddad had plunged me into. The story of Johnny Morgan would now be told.

# Chapter 3
# The Black Book

Our evening journey home was uneventful. I nodded off to sleep with the momentum of the car. It's funny that even whilst you are in that state, you have a peripheral awareness of where you are on a familiar journey. It's as if your mind remains aware of the twists and turns in the road. The three of us, if we stayed awake, would often have a competition when we were younger, to see who the best was at identifying where we were in the dark. I always knew when we had reached the Belmont roundabout because there it was so much lighter. I instinctively know when we are near home because we reach a crossroads by the BMW garage and go straight over and 100 metres on we turn up our steep drive. It's as if the bumps and lumps in the road leave an imprint on your brain!

I explained to my family that Granddad had asked me to tell the story of his life. Everyone was interested and said that they would be happy to help in any way they could. I told them that Granddad had left a book recalling his life, his army photos and some medals. I left out the jadeite stones and the bombshell about a child, as Granddad Johnny had asked me only to tell Dad certain sensitive things. My brother Liam who is eighteen months younger than me volunteered to research the medals as he is interested in joining the army when he is seventeen. So I collected Granddad's medals from the box and gave them to Liam.

The day after the funeral, I began to examine the black book. The pages were creamy without lines and were slightly curled in the outer corners. I scanned randomly leafing through from front to back. As Granddad Johnny had said, the memoirs were non-sequential and certainly did not have any reference to months or years. It became obvious as I browsed that they were divided into military and personal events. Where to begin?

I spoke to Dad about establishing a timeline for Granddad Johnny and possibly a family tree. We knew, from the front cover of the 'order of service' at his funeral that he was born on the 24 September 1925. Dad had a little think and said, "I'm sure I did a little work on a family tree when I was your age. Let me think where I put it…" A bit later, he came back with a black bible in his hand and explained that Welsh families often kept their family trees in the front of a family bible. It was a black-bound heavily veined, leather effect book with the HOLY BIBLE in gold lettering on the front but not centrally placed. Inside the front and back cover, it was black paper bound and the edges of the pages were a platinum colour and yes there was a family tree on the first white page.

My granddad was born in Dock Street, Lower Loughor. His parents were William and Annie and they had been born in 1884 and 1896 respectively. They had five children; three boys and two girls: Peggy—1918; Glenys—1920; Edward—1923; Johnny—1925; Philip—1940. William Morgan was from Lower Loughor (Glamorganshire). Annie Thomas was from Berwick Road, Bynea (Carmarthenshire).

It's strange to note that we are taught about British History in relation to the world and yet we know so little of our own family heritage. I asked Dad about Granddad's childhood and he pondered for a bit. "Well, I only know snippets of information. He passed the eleven-plus and was eligible to go to Gowerton 'Grammar School', but he couldn't go because his parents couldn't afford to send him so he started working in the local steel works at the age of 14, I believe. He was a pretty good footballer by all accounts playing for his county and having trials for Cardiff City and Swansea Town. The 'Swans' wanted to sign him, but something happened that prevented this. He was also an excellent swimmer with a very powerful and stylish front crawl. As kids, he and his siblings used to swim in the Loughor River. It is a treacherous expanse of water known for its undercurrents with quite a few fatalities from drowning."

"Dad's family are somewhat of a mystery as I never met any of them and apart from making reference to them swimming in the river that was about it. Seeing Philip at the funeral was quite a surprise as I assumed they were all dead. I know that Dad joined the army when he was seventeen."

"Hang on a minute," I requested curiously. "That would make it 1942 which is three years before the end of the Second World War."

"Dad never spoke about his military experiences," my dad continued. "He married Mum in 1964 and I was born in 1965. He's fourteen years older than my mum, you know. About a year or two after they got married, he started a club teaching all traditional Korean martial arts, which he must have learned whilst in the army. He did this as a hobby whilst also working full-time as a motor mechanic. He was extremely proud of his skills with cars, motorbikes and lawnmowers. In fact, he was good with anything that had an engine. Going back to the martial arts club, it was popular because it was so different I suppose. Because of its success, he soon became the full-time sensei. He trained my brothers and me and he continued with your generation.

"The study and practice of 'Martial arts' is the family business: purely because of him. He absolutely loved it and never felt like he was working. When those military gentlemen spoke about his role in the Korean War, I was very proud of him. I know the Korean War was in the early fifties but that's as much as I know really. I'm also astonished that he was a member of the SAS as they are considered to be amongst the most elite of Special Forces. Apart from some childhood memories, I don't know much about his previous life, sadly. He has never told me anything about the period before he met Mum and I'm pretty sure Mum doesn't know that much as she has never said."

I decided in that instant that now was the right time to tell Dad about the baby. So, with some hesitation, I said, "There's a rather sensitive issue that I need to tell you about." I whispered in a rather embarrassed way.

Dad looked at me as if to say, "What could be so embarrassing?" So, I told him about what Granddad Johnny had said about the pregnancy and all the information I had about the child and her mother. My dad's eyes opened wide with shock. He put his fist under his chin and looked at me thoughtfully, before saying, "That's a big secret to keep to yourself for all those years. He must have been weighed down heavily by it. I wonder why he never told Mam? I'm going to have to tell her at some point but so soon after the funeral is simply not appropriate. How she will react to this bombshell, I do not know. I'll have to have a good think about this. It's a pity Dad didn't let this secret out of the bag sooner as I'm sure that with my contacts at the 'Foreign Office', more research could have been done to discover whether she's alive and if she is, where she is! In fact, that might be a good idea anyway. After all, she is my half-sister!"

Dad went to make a few phone calls and half an hour later came back looking rather pleased with himself and said, "There, I have a few colleagues who will do some research into 'Mul Yong Yi!' Obviously, they will do the research in their own time, of course. Once they get started, no stone will be left unturned."

I then proceeded to tell Dad more fully about what Granddad had left in the chest: the diary, photos, medals, berets, valuable jewellery and the letter to me. Dad said, "I've always been a little puzzled about how Mum and Dad have managed over the years financially as his job didn't pay that much. Now I know that he has been selling that jadeite to fund them all these years. Each piece must be worth a lot of money! I better make sure that Mam is given the jadeite as soon as possible with an explanation of their value and how Dad has been using them over the years to finance their lifestyle. Perhaps, you could find out from the black book who Dad has been selling them to!"

After our conversation, I couldn't help wondering what Granddad Johnny had been doing between 1942 when he joined the army, and when he married my nan in 1964.

Twenty-two years of history to fill in. Apart from the mention of the Korean War, it is clear very little detail is known about where he was or what he was doing. Using the medals to ascertain his whereabouts is a distinct piece of research. Now I'm like many teenagers where history is concerned. It was more interesting in primary school as they tried hard to take us to places of interest and encouraged us to do projects on historical interests of our own choosing, and it just didn't seem so serious. Secondary school seems to take the joy out of the subject, whether it's the teacher, or just how they are expected to deliver the syllabus: I'll be honest, History isn't my favourite subject. But this project really has me enthused. I think it's personal and also the mystery about this enigmatic man has me totally hooked. Would it be different if he wasn't my grandfather? Philip Morgan, of course, would be a good new source of information as well!

Anyway, this Easter holiday, I am going to give finding out about him a good crack coupled with continuing my martial arts training. Now as you have already been informed, I practise a Korean Martial Art system that teaches combat skills such as throwing, groundwork, kicking and punching, wrestling and joint and choking holds. My dad and his two brothers, Tom and Harry had to take over from Granddad when he died suddenly. Between them, they run two martial arts schools. My uncles are in charge of the one in Llanelli and my dad is the 'sensei' in Usk, which is about fifty minutes away from Hereford. He does have some senior practitioners who take over for him when he is away, which to be quite honest is often.

I started learning at the age of five and have trained three times a week ever since. It is a very thorough process—training and then testing at every stage. I am studying for a black belt third Dan. I gained my first Dan at the age of twelve. I am proficient in many techniques—punching, kicking, choking, pressure points and joint locks being my particular favourites; although I am becoming quite adept in the use of weapons, particularly in archery and staff work. In more recent times, I have been attending martial arts classes in other disciplines, such as judo, Brazilian jujitsu, Thai boxing and the Israeli defence system, Krav Maga. I've been doing this with a view to entering a 'mixed martial arts' competition. On Wednesdays, I help out at the Usk club whilst I'm training. I usually work with primary-aged kids, which has its moments. I love it really!

In fact, on the back of my experiences with the children at the club, I am going to train to be a primary school teacher. My 'A' level exams are in May so it should be quite a busy time. Also, I have to enter three competitions every year to maintain progress in my Korean martial arts training and besides doing research on Granddad Johnny's life and revising for my 'A' levels; I will have to prepare for a 'mixed martial' arts competition.

The next morning, Philip Morgan came to visit. After his brisk knock at the door, Dad led him into the kitchen. He brought a lovely bunch of roses and a box of chocolates for my mum and gave my dad a bottle of Irish single malt whiskey. He smiled at our forlorn looks and pulled out some packets of sweets which he said he had purchased from the indoor market in Hereford. They were our favourites: chocolate-covered peanuts, chocolate-covered Brazil nuts, pink shrimps, raspberry shoe laces, wriggly worms and massive gob-stoppers. He knew how to butter us kids up! We were his friends for life! Shallow I know!

Mum put the percolator on. Now this ancient 'percolator' was the butt of many a family joke. It always seemed to take forever and made the strangest gurgling and slurping noises as if it was drinking itself whilst brewing coffee. However, for all the joking, it makes the best coffee, particularly when you add cream and 'special' short-bread guest biscuits. After twenty minutes of general chit-chat, the wonderful coffee was ready. During the waiting time, Philip apologised to Mum and Dad for his emotional behaviour the day before and said that he could not go into my nan's house as he was too upset. He would go back and give his condolences to our Nan when he felt able to. He was staying in the UK for as long as it took. He also said that he no longer had any ties so was a free agent to travel the world!

Dad and Mum were keen to hear the story of his life. I must admit us three young ones were also intrigued. So, over the heavenly-smelling and perfectly percolated coffee, he told us his story.

*As you know, I immigrated to Canada with my sister Glenys and her husband Ronnie when I was six. As I've already said, Ronnie was a mining engineer and had a job waiting for him. We went to live in a city called Whitehorse which is in the Yukon Territory in North-West Canada. Ronnie had a very high-paying job which came with a house, free private schooling for me and a health care package for the family. Glenys and Ronnie were unable to have kids so they poured all their love into me. I participated in a lot of outdoor and winter sports. I was a pretty decent downhill skier and fairly skilled at shooting and cross-country skiing. I was particularly adept at boxing and became the state champion. I attended the army cadets and was determined that I would follow my brother Johnny into the military.*

*At the age of eighteen, I left Canada and joined the United States Marine Corps. I did four years as a marine and then became a marine diver in the underwater detection team. In 1963, I became a Navy SEAL which is probably the American equivalent of the British Special Boat Service. I did tours of duty in Vietnam, Grenada and other places I'm not at liberty to mention. During the Vietnam War, I was captured by the North Vietnamese army and spent quite a bit of time being treated rather badly. I was eventually released and continued with my military career. I gained the rank of Master Chief Petty Officer in the 16 years I was with the SEALs. I was in the naval services for twenty years. On leaving the service, I was recruited into the American government's special operations group. I have never married and don't have any children. The floor is now open for questions but I must tell you, there may be some I will not answer!*

I asked a question immediately, "How come we have never met you?"

Uum…well, this is only the second time I've been to the UK since I was six. Johnny used to 'come see me' in Canada when I was younger. I suppose life just got in the way. I did see Johnny in Vietnam in '69 when he with others rescued me from a prisoner-of-war camp in Laos and then when I was 'seconded' to the regiment in Hereford for a year.

I said, "Pardon, what did you say?"

Philip replied carefully, "Which part?"

I blustered, "The part about Granddad Johnny rescuing you! I haven't read about it in his black book."

"A black book, huh, well, perhaps he didn't feel it was worthy of comment or perhaps you just haven't found it yet.

Anyway, it is what it is. Apparently, he was in the area and got wind of the fact that I had been captured. My perceived relationship with my brother is complicated and his being involved in my release, I still find rather perplexing and puzzling. Johnny was always the one for playing down his involvement in important events! As I grew older, my resentment towards Johnny grew and our not being in contact regularly probably exacerbated my feelings.

To be honest, I think that I blamed and still blame Johnny for Mum's death. It was, particularly noticeable when I became an awkward, moody teenager. I also blamed him for my moving to Canada. Deep down, I wondered why he didn't want me to stay with him instead of going with Glenys to Canada. But that question is easily rationalised. He was only eighteen and wasn't ready to have an instant family. All irrational thoughts I know but nonetheless the reasons did affect my relationship with him.

We wrote to each other occasionally at first but that fizzled out. We always sent each other Christmas and birthday cards and the occasional catch-up letter, but yes, sadly the relationship could have been closer and we both should have tried harder! On leaving the UK at the age of six, I never saw my brother Ed or sister Peggy again. Glenys kept in touch with them for a number of years but contact just 'petered' out I guess!"

I made a note in my head to seek out Philip's rescue in Vietnam because I felt sure that Granddad would have recorded this important event somewhere in the black book.

My dad then asked if his adoptive parents were still alive.

"Sadly, no! Glenys died in 2002 at the age of 82. Ronnie passed away two years later at the age of 86. I miss them a lot.

They really were the best of couples and wonderful people. They treated me as their own child. They were always loving and caring, firm but fair. They provided me with a good education, taught me about the real values of life and always looked at life in a positive way even during the worst of times. They saw themselves as Canadians and became citizens. Although, whenever Wales played Canada in rugby, they had a hard time with divided loyalties."

Mum asked an interesting question. "Does 'special operations group' mean working with or as a member of the CIA?"

"Well, it 'might' mean that! But I couldn't possibly respond in the negative or the positive. What do you both do for a living if I may ask?"

He laughed, his smile and twinkling eyes held mischief in them. The three of us looked at our parents, who fidgeted uncomfortably and smirked in unison.

Dad explained that he worked for the 'Foreign Office'; at which, Philip's smile grew wider before saying, "Ah, yes, I've come across British Foreign Office workers before. An exciting and exacting job I'm sure." Mum responded by saying she was a 'stay at home' little housewife! Dad smirked at that. It was as if the three of them had some private joke they weren't letting us kids in on. It's infuriating when adults do that!

Rhianna asked an even more interesting question, "If it's not too upsetting to respond to; what was it like being a prisoner of war during the Vietnam conflict?"

"My unit was sent to the Central Highlands of Vietnam to train an ethnic group of people by the name of the 'Montagnards' to fight the Vietcong. Working with the

Australian Army Training Team, we taught them how to disrupt the 'Ho Chi Minh Trail' which was a supply line that ran from North Vietnam through Laos and Cambodia to South Vietnam. This supply line provided weapons, manpower, ammunition and other materials to sympathisers in South Vietnam. Protestant and Catholic missionaries had converted the Montagnards to Christianity so their religious beliefs and their minority status caused tensions with the Vietnamese majority. They also did not have any interest in 'communist ideology' and seemed a good ally for the United States to cultivate. They had been coastal people who had been driven away from their lands by the influx of other ethnic groups more powerful than them.

I was captured, whilst, ironically, training the Montagnards, to prepare ambushes for the Vietcong. I had been in the country for around six months. We were taken to a camp in Laos, where I remained for three months. We were rescued by a company of the $212^{th}$, $1^{st}$ Mike (Mobile Strike and Reaction) force Battalion with helicopter support and of course, my dear brother Johnny had to tag along. Many of my comrades died during those three months and I lost half my body weight due to lack of food and continuous torture.

It has taken me a fair few years to unravel my feelings about my time in captivity. As you can imagine, being a 'prisoner' of any kind first of all removes your freedom to determine what you will or will not do. Secondly, it confines you to an area defined by others. Others determine when you wash, go to the toilet, eat, drink or have exercise. The power you once had is in the hands of someone else. Now couple this with an enemy that hates you; an enemy, that on a daily basis, will do anything in his power to break you physically, mentally and psychologically.

I was tortured and starved. They were also quick to remove those basic human rights that I've already mentioned for the slightest perceived misdemeanour. They tried to make me criticise the USA for interfering in Vietnam. They were not really interested in any information I may have had to give. They wanted you to feel helpless and hopeless. They wanted you to be submissive and submit to their will. They wanted to degrade and debase you so you thought of yourself as worthless and unfit to exist. The North Vietnamese and the Vietcong did not bother to take the ordinary soldier prisoner. They just killed them horribly. I was an officer. They kept officers as trophies to be used for negotiations later in the war. Many did not survive. Many who did survive committed suicide at a later date because they had been so traumatised by their treatment. Those who avoided the path of suicide found it difficult to sustain and make long-term relationships. There were high rates of divorce, drug and alcohol dependence and extreme forms of violence for many of those who survived. It was 'post-traumatic stress disorder' before the illness had been labelled or recognised. They had been dehumanised and whilst they appeared 'normal' on the outside they were rabid animals on the inside! As you can see by the way I speak about it, I still have some unresolved issues."

Philip stopped at that point and said with a sad smile, "Clearly, I am a long way off putting some of my past experiences behind me. I'll get off my soap-box! Sorry, everyone. I didn't mean to burden you with my emotional outbursts. After a great deal of self-reflection, one thing I do understand is how extreme events in your life can contribute to catastrophic outcomes for yourself and those you love. Perhaps, I have chosen to live a solitary life because I don't want to burden others with my psychological problems. However, I've come closer to understanding what was going on in my father's mind all those years ago and that the fear generated in nightmares that never go away can be transcribed to reality in a fleeting tragic moment. With those thoughts, I will now stop talking."

What Philip had told us about himself made him appear far more 'human'. He had become more real in my eyes and I liked him even more because he showed his vulnerability. I have to say though; he is very much like Granddad Johnny to my way of thinking! Although he is probably more open about his inner feelings than Granddad ever was.

Philip had booked into the 'Castle House Hotel' for a few nights and asked us if we would all like to join him for dinner, the following evening; 'his treat'. Mum and Dad graciously accepted the offer much to our relief. Dad went on to add, "I'm not sure if you three have the time or inclination to come along. What do you think?"

The three of us replied in unison, "We'll be there!"

The following evening, we ordered a taxi down to the hotel. Philip showed us his room, which was extremely opulent, before going down to dinner. We had drinks in their small but beautiful bar. I had a glass of medium white wine, as did Mum. Dad and Philip each had a pint of the 'Wye Valley Butty Bach' whilst Liam was allowed a half of beer. Poor Rhianna was only allowed a soft drink, although Mum did give her a sip of her wine. Philip Morgan was a jolly person with a very witty, dry nature. We ate, drank and laughed at his stories. The three adults all had too much alcohol and the evening flew by in a blur. Time always seems to pass too quickly when you are enjoying yourself. Mum and Dad invited Philip up for coffee the next day.

Over coffee the following morning, Dad explained about the Korean child Granddad and Mi Yong had and that he was going to try to find her. He also explained that he hadn't told his mum about the child yet. He was plucking up the courage to do so. He also mentioned the 'black book' that Granddad had left me. Philip was very curious about the book and asked if he could have a look sometime. Philip also offered to contact a few of his American sources. After all, Mul Yong was his niece! Mum and Dad asked him how long he would be staying in the UK. He wasn't certain but he did intend to visit Scotland and Southern Ireland to catch up with some old friends. We were sad to see him go. He did say that if we needed his help with anything, he was quite willing to be of assistance.

The following morning, I collected the 'black book' from the ornate box hidden under my bed and went into our study/office. I started once again skimming pages and I came across a section that drew my interest:

*Twilight—guarding the Imjin River crossing against Chinese and North Korean infantry. Stillness—as if the world was watching in trepidation at the expected violence. Our seventeen-man patrol from 7 platoon C company—the Glosters lay with bated breath on the fifteen-foot high river bank overlooking the shingle beach that would be the easiest crossing point. The Imjin is a very wide river. On the far bank, a single enemy soldier appeared in silhouette looking cautiously up and down the far bank before stepping into the rippling, inky black water. The full moon reflected eerily off the obsidian black surface. He took two strides into the thigh-high water constantly turning his head from side to side, cradling his weapon chest high out of the water, alert to any sign of enemy movement. He took another two steps, the river current making it difficult to stand. He stopped rigidly still, took a deep breath, listened carefully for another long moment, and then lifted his right arm in a fist to signal for the others well hidden in the bushes to move forward.*

*The amount of enemy soldiers filing silently into the black water was alarming and unexpected. When the lead scout reached over three-quarters of the way across the river, the ambush was sprung; flares shot up, lighting the river like a Guy Fawkes firework display back home.*

*Rapid single-shot fire from Lee Enfield rifles and staccato hammering of Bren guns echoed across the river. The Chinese soldiers making the crossing were easy targets and many bodies were seen floating away on the swift-moving current with others closer to the far bank making a terrified retreat. The return fire came in the form of a machine gun high up on the far bank; its green tracer arching across the intervening space and burp guns making their characteristic belching sound on firing. At this point, we were ordered to pull back in good order. My role with others was to provide covering fire until the rest had moved to our next firing position. As I rose, ready to back away, positioned as I was, near the edge of the river bank, I felt a pull on my right shoulder and an excruciating burning pain. I felt myself knocked backwards with the force but then instinctively pushed myself forward to avoid falling, only to overcompensate and thus fall head-first into the blackness of the river.*

*My weapon slipped from my grasp as I hit the water. The splash seemed tremendously loud and I plunged down, deep into the murkiness; I panicked with cold shock and struck out for the surface. On reaching the surface, I gasped for air. The water was fast-moving. I managed to turn onto my back and just floated along with the current. I felt my right shoulder to establish the extent of the wound and heaved a sigh inwardly as the fingers of my left hand explored the area. No entry or exit wound, but a bloodied groove along the muscle above the clavicle where the round had traced its path. It had shredded my tunic. Just a bloody graze as the platoon sergeant would have said sarcastically. I had to get the ammunition pouches off me as they had become saturated and were pulling me inexorably down. I undid the buckle around my waist and heaved first one shoulder and then the wounded shoulder out of the shoulder straps, grimacing with pain. I released and they sank immediately. The noise of battle drifted away as my floating body was driven by the current into the centre of the river.*

*There were Chinese bodies around me and I collided with a few making me shudder involuntarily at the coldness of death. Some floated face down whilst others stared lifelessly at the winking myriad of stars in the night sky, never to view the universe again. What a terrible waste of life and at that moment, I regretted all the years I had fought for my country! I could not manoeuvre myself towards either bank as the torrent was too strong; I just had to be patient and go with the flow. After what seemed like an age, a bend in the river slowed the current down bringing a more sedate water movement and*

*I was able to scull towards shore using leg strokes and my one good arm. I attempted to feel for the bottom with my feet and stood up with a start. It was just up to my knees and I was able to wade out. The cold and wet were beginning to make my teeth chatter and I knew I had to find shelter soon or I would begin to start suffering from hypothermia.*

*I left the river and moved up into the tree line. I gathered some ferns from the undergrowth and went back to the sandy area that I had come ashore at and obliterated my footprints whilst carefully moving backwards to the safety of the trees. I settled behind an immense rhododendron tree and took my battle uniform off; which consisted of a dark blue beret, blouse, shirt, tie and trousers; yes, we went into battle wearing a tie, and then took off my heavy black boots with canvas anklets. I kept my underpants on just in case I was caught by the enemy unexpectedly. The ground around me was covered in ferns so I gathered fronds of ferns and covered myself in their layers in an attempt to gain warmth and provide cover. It was eerily quiet in the woods and after a short while, I stopped shivering and nodded off to sleep.*

The account stopped at that point and I turned the page over to read further but it was an account of something else completely unconnected. I'm sure that he resumed his commentary somewhere else in the black book and I would look for it again later. But I had to stop at that point as my heart was racing and I was gnawing the nails on my right hand subconsciously. He was lucky to be alive. I sighed heavily, closed the book, and placed it back in the box before storing it away in my wardrobe.

I 'Face Timed' Nan after lunch! I asked her how she had met Granddad Johnny. I told her about going out for an evening meal with Granddad's brother Philip. She was curious about that and I explained how the evening had gone. She was pleased that he had visited us but we soon got back to the reason why I was calling. She was quite happy to recall the first time they had met. It was called a 'Twmpath Dawns' which was popular in the 1950s and 1960s. Basically, a Welsh barn dance, where young people met and live music played. It was the autumn of 1962 when Nan was 22 years old. She said that Granddad wasn't much of a 'talker' and that he was very slim but muscular. He had almost jet-black hair, green eyes and a strong jawline with a cute dimple chin. He approached her shyly for a dance and the night then flew by so quickly. They arranged to meet the next day and their courtship lasted two years before marrying in 1964.

What did she know about him I asked. Well, when she met him, he was a soldier and spent considerable lengths of time away but he was reluctant to talk about it, dismissing it as the 'follies of youth' and a foolish profession. She did say that he had been traumatised by his experiences. "How did you know that?" I asked.

"Well, there was sadness about him when we first started going out and he could be a little grumpy and gloomy. He soon cheered up after going out with me a few times," my nan said forcefully. "He didn't say too much about his family, although he did say he had brothers and sisters. I just assumed that there had been a family disagreement and that he had distanced himself from them. It was shocking to hear from his brother about what happened to his mum and dad. What a terrible thing for a young man to witness and I'm surprised he never talked to me about it. He must have been really traumatised by the event."

I asked Nan about her own family and what they thought about her and Granddad's developing relationship. She was quiet for a moment, before saying, "Well, Bach, you may be surprised to know this, but I come from a Romany Gipsy family and our culture does not look favourably on 'outsiders'. So, it was difficult. We lived in caravans on a site in Burry Port. My 'Da' was a bit handy with his fists and his belt. He had a very short fuse and would become violent very quickly. I am the youngest of nine and was the last one living at home when I started going out with Johnny. I couldn't pluck up the courage to tell them that I was going out with him as that would have caused ructions.

Anyway, they did find out and it did cause unpleasantness with my Da knocking me about a bit and threatening me with even worse if I saw Johnny again. I remember meeting Johnny the following evening as I didn't accept bullying from anyone, and him noticing that my arms and face were black and blue. I had tried to conceal the bruising on my face with make-up but Johnny noticed. I obviously had to explain to him about my Da's temper and why he had knocked me about. He was enraged. I tried to brush it off as nothing for him to worry about. Anyway, we carried on with our evening and he dropped me off later that night. As I walked away, Johnny said in a loud, clear voice that my father would not be knocking me about again and just got on his bike and drove away.

When Da came home from work the next day, he had clearly been in a fight. His nose was mashed and he had two black eyes. He didn't say a word about it when we sat down for our evening meal. Two of my uncles came around later and they looked as if they had had good hiding too! My Ma told me that the three of them had got into a fight in the carpark of a local pub with a stranger and had come out second best.

I met Johnny the next day and I asked him if he had been knocking my father and uncles about. He just smiled shyly but didn't say anything. He didn't have a mark on him! Correction, he did have some redness on both his knuckles. Romany gipsy men are not quick to forgive but they do admire aggression and courage. After a proper length of time 'courting', we decided to get married at the town registry office. My Ma gave me away and my older twin sisters attended but there were no male members of my family present."

She said that although Granddad Johnny wasn't a chatty person, he was kind, had a good, intelligent sense of humour, and was considerate; caring deeply for her right from the start. He had a motorbike, a Royal Enfield 'Constellation' which was a twin-cylinder 700cc bike which weighed around 425lbs and could do more than 110mph and on it, they used to travel to all the local beauty spots. Apparently, he kept the bike nice and shiny and did all the maintenance himself. It was his pride and joy.

I looked at her in amazement and said, "How do you remember all the bike details, Nan?"

"Well, 'Bach', that was one of the few things your granddad Johnny would talk about for hours on end so I must have taken some of it in. Yes, I was a real 'biker chick', what with the leathers and the matt black crash helmet. With the wind in your face and the hedge-rows rushing passed, it felt thrilling and so good to be alive." She described a motorbike accident they had been in—the wheels of the bike slipping on an oil slick, the bike pinning them both down until Granddad had pulled himself out realising that Nan was more seriously injured than he had thought. The pillion foot rest had gone through her left ankle and the weight of the bike was pressing down through the wound. She said the pain was agonising and that she must have passed out.

Granddad flagged down a passing motorist and they managed to lift the bike with Nan still attached so that the weight of the bike on the wound was reduced. In the meantime, someone had called for the fire-brigade and an ambulance. Nan showed me the scar which was pretty impressive. The fire-brigade had to cut the foot rest from the bike, whilst leaving it sticking out both sides of the ankle. She was operated on to have the rest removed. After coming out of hospital, the wound would not heal and was in the first stages of becoming gangrenous so she had to be operated on again with the wound being opened up. They found that bits from the fur-lining of her boot had not all been removed and that was causing further infection.

I looked at her with serious respect and said incredulously, "You must have been a pretty tough woman!"

She said matter-of-factly, "I still am lovely!" It is surprising, well not really, but young people have preconceptions of the elderly. Because someone is old doesn't mean to say they have always been old and haven't led interesting lives. I quizzed Nan further about Granddad's military exploits, especially about dates and the Korean War experience. She was as surprised as the rest of us by the military men at the funeral and stated that Granddad was never forthcoming about his army experiences. She did vaguely remember his best man Tom Bonilla but said that she had only met him that once and it was a very long time ago.

Granddad's experiences before they met were complete mysteries to her and she had not dwelt on his past but on their future together. So, I had found some general background to his life, but little to go on about his life prior to meeting my nan. I had a number of strands yet to explore: Tom Bonilla would be able to inform me further about Granddad Johnny's exploits during the Korean War; he could also point me in the right direction as to what Granddad did whilst in the army prior to his time in Korea. That evening, I leafed through the black book again and found the following account.

# Chapter 4
# The Attack

*I trudged wearily down the litter-strewn main street returning from the one and only antique shop in the market town I have called home for off and on of seventy-eight years. I felt a little down-hearted with regard to what the antique owner had offered me for the precious goods I carried in the left breast pocket of my coat. The pain in my right shoulder, caused by a wound inflicted during the Korean War, caused me to walk with my shoulder pushing forward stiffly causing my musculature and skeleton to be out of alignment; the body ache being fairly intolerable. It caused me to rock my upper body in a continuous shrugging motion.*

*Within yards of leaving the antique shop, I placed my hand in the inside left breast pocket of my jacket, checking once again that the precious, valuable objects I carried were safely ensconced. I had been so absorbed by this that I failed to notice immediately the three youths standing in a shop doorway shivering in the cold morning light. They saw me struggling along the pavement on their side of the road and I immediately felt a sense of threat and my instincts were rarely wrong. As I approached, they left the doorway and moved casually towards me.*

"Hey, old man, get any money from the antique shop?" A tall, skinny kid with a spotty face, growled threateningly.

"None of your business if I did, son," I stated plainly.

"Now that's not very charitable when we are obviously in need," laughed the stockiest and shortest of the three.

"We are going to beat you senseless unless you hand over all you have on you," said the gangly kid with the ginger hair, in a menacing tone. I smiled at his bluster and that seemed to infuriate him. "What you smiling at, old man?" He raged.

"I was just thinking how your friends will react when you tell them a seventy-eight-year-old granddad gave you a good hiding. You may be taking on more than you realise," I stated seriously. This made the three of them glance at each other and snigger loudly. I decided to reason with them further and said, "Look, lads, I don't want any trouble and it would be wise to take heed of what I'm about to say. You will probably find this amusing but I have been trained in unarmed combat and I really don't want to hurt any of you." With that, the three started roaring with laughter, which I suppose wasn't unexpected considering they assumed that an old guy would not be able to deal with three opponents.

The tall skinny kid grinned and stated enthusiastically, "You're just a joke, old man and as you think you're so amusing, we are going to make you sorry you ever came out of the old people's home this morning." He nodded at the ginger-haired lad who moved quickly to grab me by the lapels of my jacket and shove me towards a shop window. I anticipated the action and turned myself away from the window so I had room to manoeuvre.

"I'll give you one more chance to walk away so think carefully," I said through gritted teeth. He smiled at that, *releasing one arm from the hold he had on my front and pulled his arm back to punch me. Whenever I fight, everything seems to come into sharp focus and actions around me seem to move in slow motion. I saw the blow coming and stepped inside whilst moving even closer to him. The blow missed my head. I whispered, "You really don't want to do this!" before using his forward momentum to unbalance him. I then reacted aggressively: speed, strength and ruthlessness were now essential elements for my defence. Both arms came up instinctively and dipped under the youth's wrists, then I grabbed and twisted them without letting go; the youth leaned forward with a shout of pain and anger and at that moment, I butted him forcefully in the face. He screamed in agony and dropped to the ground holding his bloody, battered face.*

*Startled into action the tall, skinny youth moved to attack me by throwing a punch at my face. I ducked beneath the intended blow, grabbed and twisted the lapel of the lad's coat with my right hand whilst my left gripped his right elbow; at that point, I dipped my right hip low and forcefully into his body and turned away explosively. His forward momentum took him over my right shoulder and he landed in a crumpled heap on the hard, unyielding pavement. I did not let him go at that point but checked that he was no longer a threat to me. He seemed stunned by the turn of events and very winded by the whole experience. I straightened up from my crouch and turned to the remaining youth: the short, stocky lad who had remarked about charity and need.*

*"Come on, lad, it's your turn to have a go. Let's see if you're made of sterner stuff than your two mates, eh? I'll give you all a bit of free advice though. Firstly, never underestimate the enemy. Secondly, you had more of a chance*

*if you had attacked me together and not individually. Finally, and most importantly, when you commit to an action you must follow it through no matter what the pain."* The short, stocky lad with eyes gawking and an ashen face did not respond but turned and ran. Without a backward glance, I continued on my way; although any onlooker would have noticed that I seemed to stand taller and walk in a more confident, assertive way and I certainly had a twinkle in my eye.

When I arrived home, I told my wife about the attack and she was horrified. She insisted I phone the police and notify them about the attack. This I did, having to give my name, address and telephone number to the polite, female telephonist on the other end of the line. About an hour later, a police car pulled up in our drive and a young police officer came to the door. My wife led him into the lounge where I was sitting watching TV. The conversation was fairly brief with the policeman stating that I needed to go with him to the police station as there had been an allegation of assault made against me. I cringed inside and nodded in agreement that it needed to be cleared up. We both climbed into the police vehicle and proceeded to the police station.

On arrival, I was placed in a drab, poky interview room and waited for someone to come and take my statement. Eventually, the young policeman returned with a more senior detective. The senior officer introduced himself as Detective Williams and then began by asking that I confirm my name, address and telephone number. Then he asked me to explain what happened from my point of view. This I did succinctly. The young police officer wrote down what I had said and asked me to sign and date the statement. *"How old are you, Mr Morgan?"* Detective Williams asked curiously.

"Well, let me think...I'm seventy-eight."

Detective Williams went on to say, "The youth who made the complaint said that you attacked him as he was standing looking in a shop window. Is there any reason you would do that? Do you know him from somewhere?"

I replied, "No, I've never seen him before and as I said there were three of them not just the one."

"I'm afraid we will have to look into this matter a little further, Mr Morgan. We will be in touch and please don't worry as I'm sure we can clear this up quickly," Detective Williams stated reassuringly whilst patting me on the shoulder.

The next day I had a visit from Detective Williams whilst I was working on my vegetable plot. He asked me if I had a DVD player which I confirmed with a nod of the head, and if would I be kind enough to come inside and view a CCTV recording he had retrieved from a camera in the street. He put it on and we viewed the scene where I was attacked by the two boys with another looking on.

Detective Williams seemed to watch the events unfolding with a wry smile. "Mr Morgan, I've watched this video a number of times with colleagues at the police station and it is quite clear that you were attacked by two young men. You did not initiate any assault by words or actions so therefore the allegation of assault against you cannot proceed. You have nothing to answer for. Two of the young men have been charged with assault and the third for aiding and abetting a criminal act. These young men have only recently come out of a youth offenders institution for other acts of violence. After questioning, they did admit that you had warned them about your unarmed combat expertise. Clearly, they should have *listened. Thank you for being so cooperative and honest. Our job would be much simpler if there were more people like you. It is also very lucky that you warned them about your combat experience in an attempt to defuse the situation as without that warning you might have initiated a more in-depth investigation into your actions.*

*Unfortunately, when the young men have to go to court for the assault you will have to attend and give your version of events. It's nothing to be worried about as the CCTV evidence is compelling. Mr Morgan, how is it that you are so accomplished in self-defence?" I told him about my martial arts school. On his way out, he shook my hand warmly and said, "Mr Morgan, I would just like to say that it has been my privilege to meet you." I then went into the kitchen to put the kettle on and sighed with relief. That was that. Or so I thought.*

*When he left, my wife Mil told me that whilst Detective Williams had been waiting for me to come in from the garden she had asked him if I was in trouble. He laughed and said, "When I looked at the CCTV footage of the attack I was so astonished that I started clapping. Don't get me wrong, Mrs Morgan, I obviously cannot condone violence but this was an exceptional incident. I had to keep replaying the footage because it was so amazing that one person could deal with those thugs. A seventy-eight-year-old is even more incredible! By the time I had finished, a crowd of police officers and other personnel were also viewing the action. At the end of each replay, there was a spontaneous round of applause and whoops of delight. Your husband is one tough customer not to be messed with."*

*My wife had replied, "Oh, I already knew that!"*

*Unfortunately, the local press, namely the 'Llanelli Mercury', got wind of the incident and I had quite a few reporters knocking at the front door asking for an interview. I am not a person seeking the public glare and courteously refused all requests.*

*Mildred suggested that the reporters would leave me alone if I was to give an exclusive to one of them so I relented. The following week the article appeared on the front page of the local newspaper under the headline: PENSIONER PULVERISES TEENAGE PREDATORS. I was so embarrassed. Friends, family, my students and neighbours all congratulated me for standing up to the thugs and I was also ribbed mercilessly by the same people. I was convinced that it would soon blow over but I was wrong. Somehow, it reached the national press; was reported in many of the tabloid and broadsheet newspapers and to my eternal consternation, I was invited to appear on Breakfast Television on ITV and the BBC. I cordially refused any further intrusions into my private life and it did eventually cease being newsworthy to my great relief. I did have to give evidence in court a number of months later and the lads were sent to prison for a year.*

It did not surprise me that Granddad was able to do that to those young hooligans. He was after all a master of martial combat. He had been instructing martial arts for over fifty years and had travelled to many far-flung places to take classes and enter competitions. He never boasted about his expertise, but even at his advanced age, he could handle himself in difficult situations. He must have been a force of nature as a young man. As for the press—well, it must have been quite exciting but clearly overwhelming for Granddad as he was a very private person. I was only seven at the time and have no memory of the entire event. The opening paragraph of this account had also given me information as to 'who' Granddad had been selling the jadeite to. I must tell Dad!

The following day, I emailed Tom Bonilla and asked him if he could tell me what he knew about Granddad Johnny. I then went online and researched the 'Korean War', 'SAS', and a military group called 'The White Tigers'.

## This is What I Found Out About the Korean War

On 25 June 1950, the North Korean army invaded the south by crossing the 38th parallel. The South Korean army was driven back through their own capital Seoul. Member states of the United Nations, of which Great Britain was one, were asked to support the south with the USA playing a lead part. The US army was unable to contain the North Korean offensive at first and was forced back into the Pusan peninsula. The first two British regiments: namely 1st Battalions of the Middlesex; Argyll & Sutherland Highlanders; became involved, landing on 25 August 1950. Eventually, there was a breakout from the Pusan perimeter and although the North Koreans fought furiously, they were driven back beyond the 38th parallel and the capital of the north, Pyongyang fell on 20 October. The UN offensive continued north with the intention of reaching the Yalu River and the Manchurian border. At this stage, the Chinese became involved and attacked as allies of North Korea.

200,000 Chinese peasant soldiers, well used to winter conditions, forced a retreat of the UN forces. The Chinese and the Soviet Union, both communist countries, came in on the side of the north. The Soviets provided military advisers and military equipment whilst the Chinese asked their people to volunteer to fight for communism against the decadent western powers. The Gloucestershire (Glosters) arrived in Korea in November 1950. So Granddad Johnny must also have arrived then. The Battle of the Imjin River took place from the 22–25 April 1951 and from what my research suggests Granddad Johnny went into the river wounded on the 22 as the light faded.

The Imjin River skirmish, in which Granddad Johnny fell into the river and was swept away, was immediately followed by the battle for hill 235 or what came to be known as 'Gloster Hill'. Of 657 soldiers of the Gloucester regiment, only 63 reached safety; over 500 were taken prisoner by the Chinese; 58 were killed during the battle; 30 died whilst in captivity. For three days, the regiment held back the 63rd Chinese Army in their attempt to drive through to Seoul. During this battle, the Chinese sustained 11,000 casualties which were 40% of their strength. The commander of the 8th Army, Van Fleet, stated that the Glosters' action was: 'the most outstanding example of unit bravery in modern warfare' and the regiment was honoured with a US Presidential Citation. Well, Granddad Johnny seemed fated to miss all of that but I'm sure that what followed must have put him in great danger to.

The war lasted 2 years and 11 months ending with an armistice on 25 July 1953. The loss of men on both sides of the conflict was huge. Between 360,000 and 750,000 North Korean/Chinese died in the conflict. The South Koreans lost

138,000 approximately. The United Nations forces lost 178,500. The British sent 14,198 military personnel to the Korean Peninsula of which: 1,109 were killed; 2,674 were wounded; 179 were deemed 'Missing in Action' (presumed dead); 977 were taken as prisoners of war.

The Korean War is neglected by many as a conflict of little consequence and probably rightly so but the loss of life and immeasurable suffering that took place does not reflect the supposed insignificance of the event. In fact, there are still many participants of the conflict who still suffer to this day as a result of this dispute that started over sixty-eight years ago. The civilian population of South Korea were decimated by 991,000 approximately. The civilian population of North Korea lost 1,550,000. A staggering loss of life!

To this day, North Korea remains a secretive and isolated country and has never signed a peace treaty. So, where was Granddad after he went into the Imjin River on 22 April 1951?

The SAS or Special Air Service came to international prominence in May 1980 when terrorists held 26 hostages at gunpoint in the Iranian embassy in London. The events were televised around the world and this secretive special force became world renowned for its effectiveness in counter-terrorist operations. The SAS were formed during the Second World War by David Sterling and were tasked with working behind enemy lines in small groups. They were to disrupt enemy supply lines, attack airfields and rail links and generally force front-line troops to watch their backs. The SAS was disbanded for a time after the war but reinstated as a regiment from 1950 until the present day.

There are three component regiments of the SAS: 21st SAS (Artists), 23rd SAS (Territorial), 22nd SAS: 21st and

23rd are reservists. 22nd SAS regiment has been based in Hereford since 1960 and has four squadrons—A, B, D and G. There are approximately sixty men in a squadron. Apparently, 21 SAS had a three-month training exercise in preparation for Korea but were pulled out at the last minute and deployed to Malaya as there was a communist insurgency threatening the peace of the country. The overall commander in chief of the armed forces sent to Korea, Douglas MacArthur, felt that 'Special Forces' did not have a useful role to play in Korea because of the distinct differences between the population and the obvious western features of the 'Special Forces'.

The motto of the regiment is: 'Who dares wins'. Their cap badge is a 'winged dagger' and their beret is coloured beige. Now I'm sure Granddad also had a maroon beret as well with that badge on. In more recent times, the SAS were active in Oman, the Falklands and the First Gulf War locating 'scud' missiles and destroying them in Iraq; chasing 'Osama bin Laden' in the Tora-Bora Mountains of Afghanistan; countering the threat of IEDs (Improvised Explosive Devices) by locating and destroying their distribution structure in both Iraq and Afghanistan; capturing or neutralising the leaders of known terrorist organisations in Iraq, Afghanistan, Libya and latterly Syria.

In fact, the SAS has been deployed on secretive missions all over the world without the glare of the media at times, rescuing kidnapped soldiers in Sierra Leone and rescuing aid workers in Iraq and Afghanistan. There is also a rather mysterious E squadron based in Newport who works predominantly for MI6. Having done this research, I have a suspicion that my dad Alan has some connection with this secretive regiment, although there has never been any sign of military equipment of any type in our house. Perhaps, because of his job at the 'foreign office', he was obliged to visit their facility in Hereford. I think I'll have a chat with him about what his real job is all about! I wonder if he will tell me anything.

The White Tigers, given the code name 'donkey4', were a North Korean nationalist partisan group of 4000 units who had sympathy for their southern countrymen and women and were vehemently opposed to communism and Chinese influence. When the Americans realised that there were anti-government groups in the north they sent advisers to help coordinate resistance and train them in unconventional warfare. They were active from 1951–1954. They were called the United Nations Partisan Infantry Korea (UNPIK) and research suggests that their efforts at guerrilla warfare occupied 35,000 North Korean and Chinese forces. Granddad Johnny was one of the advisers. Their activity was overseen by the 8240th unit US army intelligence group based in Seoul. After the conflict, the US did not know what to do with the partisans so handed over responsibility to the South Korean military. The military was suspicious of the motives of the partisans and the integration wasn't successful. So the partisans dispersed; some moved to the south, others returned quietly to where they had originated from in the north and another group found their way to the United States, predominantly California.

The lady that Granddad Johnny had rescued and later had a child with was part of this partisan group. Life must have been very difficult for poor 'Water Dragon' after her mum had been killed. I wonder if she is still alive.

My brother Liam had also been busy and had tracked down the names of the 11 medals and what campaigns they had been awarded for and when. It did strike me as odd as I thought Granddad had mentioned 12!

1939–1945 Star (Second World War)
1939–1945 War Medal (Second World War)
1945–1948 General Service Medal with Palestine Clasp
1950–1953 Korean War Service Medal
1950–1953 United Nations Service Medal Korea
1954 Military Cross (for Korean campaign)
1950–1954 Korean Partisan Honour Medal
1954 US Army Distinguished Service Cross
1948–1960 General Service Medal with Malaya Clasp
1957–1966 Pingat Jasa Malaysia Medal
1957–1960 General Service Medal with Arabian Peninsula Clasp

So, we have information about his military activity during those intervening years but as Liam said to me, "We don't know how long his tour of duty was in any of the campaigns he gained medals from."

I received the following email from Tom Bonilla that evening:

*Dear Kerry,*

*Thank you for contacting me so soon after your Granddad's funeral. It was a very sad day, although it did bring into sharp focus for me and the others what Johnny did for so many people. We all thought you spoke very well at the funeral showing a maturity and confidence way beyond your years. The guy who spoke before me was a retired brigadier general in the British Army by the name of Harry Thomas. He was captured whilst trying to break out from Gloster Hill. He was in the same prisoner camp as me and we knew each other quite well from our attempts at escape. He has said that he would willingly give you information about Johnny's military career if you so require. The appearance of Johnny's younger brother after all those years must have been a shock to the whole family! The trauma of seeing his mother killed must have remained with Johnny all his life. Terribly sad!*

*I still have nightmares about my time as a prisoner of war, even though it was well over sixty years ago. I was a member of the USA 65th Infantry Regiment which was mainly made up of Puerto Rican soldiers with a smattering of other Hispanic groups. We were called The Borinqueneers, a name given to us after a friendly indigenous tribe in Puerto Rica. I, amongst others, was captured whilst covering the retreat of the 1st US Marine Division during the battle of Choisin Reservoir.*

*I was in a POW camp situated deep inside North Korea. It was a hard labour camp known as the caves, where we worked for 14-hour shifts digging and pick-axing iron ore whilst being given very little food. The conditions were so severe and the treatment so brutal that many American, Puerto Rican, Belgian, British and South Korean prisoners died. As I said at Johnny's funeral, we had given up hope. The rescue was very simple in its execution although it had been thoroughly prepared and researched—nothing was left to chance. In fact, we didn't even know we were being rescued until we reached a transfer point many miles away. Your granddad, working with North Korean partisans and some*

*Chinese colleagues he had brought over from Malaya, managed to procure 12 transport lorries and the correct paperwork necessary for their use and our release. The bogus officers and men allocated for the prisoner transfer had the correct uniforms, spoke the right North Korean dialect, had the right look for the escape convoy and obviously played their roles to perfection.*

*The planning had been so extensive that they were able to intercept a telephone call to the regional headquarters asking for verification that the prisoners were to be transferred. The transfer went ahead simply because the intercepted phone call reply appeared so genuine and was wholly believed by the camp administration. An excellent piece of deception by any stretch of the imagination! We only knew that we had been rescued when we were being transferred by a fishing boat to a British warship, HMS Corsair, a C-class destroyer, off the west coast of North Korea. There was plentiful air cover provided by American Mustangs and Commonwealth fighters. We were informed by an officer aboard the ship who the mastermind behind the rescue was. I later met your granddad in the ship's galley over a meal of sausage and mash—a very British concoction which I now have as part of my weekly diet—and thanked him for the rescue. He told me that it had been his last and most challenging mission behind enemy lines. He also informed me that a number of his partisan team had been killed in the complex preparation and extraction.*

*Before the Korean conflict, Johnny had been working as an instructor of jungle warfare in Malaya for a Special Forces group. In all, the POW rescue had saved one hundred and eighteen men. He told me that he could not give details on the mission as it was top secret. Over the next days and weeks whilst on board, I gradually got to know your enigmatic granddad and was amazed by his humbleness and sense of duty. He had a sharp, dry sense of humour but was really a very quiet man! The other prisoners became aware of what Johnny had done for them and one night in the galley they all sang For he's a jolly good fellow…and from there on, he was treated as if he was royalty by the crew and the prisoners he rescued.*

*He was plainly embarrassed by all the attention and said that others had done much more and even given their lives for the rescue to be successful. He was so overwhelmed by the attention that he attempted to avoid meal times from then until we docked. Instead, people went looking for him and cajoled him to eat with them. We kept in touch by letter and I was at your grandparents' wedding and had the honour of being his best man. I do know he deservedly received awards of a military cross from the British forces and a distinguished service cross from the US Army for the POW rescue. Some people might argue that the British military authorities did not recognise his heroism during numerous operations enough!*

*Kind regards*
*Tom*

*My reply:*
*Thanks, Tom for that information! I am curious though about what you did before being rescued because Granddad Johnny told me in his letter that you had escaped from a POW camp. Would it be too terrible for you to tell me about that*

*experience? Also, were you aware that Granddad had a child with one of the North Korean partisans? May I also have Harry Thomas' email address?*
*Best wishes*
*Kerry*

*Later that evening, his reply came:*

Dear Kerry,

I escaped from a previous POW camp relatively easily as the North Koreans were of the belief that prisoners would not get very far moving in a hostile environment where they would be recognised as foreigners. Fortunately, for me, my Mexican heritage makes me short in stature; I have relatively dark skin, almost black eyes, jet-black hair and look quite similar to the Korean race. Believe it or not, I took a uniform from a North Korean guard who had drunk himself into a stupor whilst on duty. There must have been quite a furore when they discovered the guy in his underwear when the relief guard came on duty. I just walked out through the main gates. I still chuckle to myself about it at odd times.

I managed to travel nearly to the coast before I was caught. I laid up in hiding during the day and travelled at night. On a few occasions, I came into contact with locals and pretended I was dumb and a little insane; pointing to my mouth and grunting seemed to work most of the time. The peasant farmers were generous with their food and water which seemed surprising as they had so little for even their own families. My subterfuge came to an end when I walked accidentally into a North Korean army camp late at night groggy with dehydration. I was beaten rather badly and *interrogated as to where I had come from in the region. During the interrogations, I spoke Spanish which really confused them. They eventually became bored with my presence and sent me to the caves where all the prisoners who attempted escape were sent—to die, I believe.*

*With regards to your other question! No, I didn't know about your granddad's child. It must have been painful emotionally for him all those years. Does Mildred know about his daughter?*

*Kind regards*
*Tom*

He also added the email address of the other gentleman who gave the eulogy at the funeral. Tom's final question made me feel very uncomfortable. Dad would have to tell Nan soon. Oh dear! How will she react?

My thoughts went to Nan. She had been married to Granddad for fifty-four years. They had three children, seven grandchildren; a whole lifetime together! What had been revealed by the 'black book' was a different life; a life that we did not know existed. Admittedly, in a different time but even so, a past history cannot remain hidden forever, particularly when you reveal it to someone! Why didn't he just tell Nan? It would have been so much easier. How would I feel if my husband had kept such a massive secret from me? I wondered why he would do that. Knowing my granddad Johnny the way I did, it didn't feel like something he would do—walk away from one thing and keep the truth hidden!

Perhaps, I didn't understand the context of the history of social development. Today, people live together, have children together, and there is not the social stigma that was prevalent in previous decades. Marriage is no longer looked upon as the only way for couples to be together. Unmarried mothers were institutionalised and their children taken away from them back in the 50s and 60s and regarded as fallen women. Being ashamed of what he had done seemed to be the only reason I could put the secrecy down to. A possible other reason might be that he did not have any hope of finding Mul Yong so thought what was the point of upsetting Nan? Anyway, it's probably a combination of both!

The following morning, whilst relaxing in bed, I retrieved the black book from under my bed, where I had started storing it for my convenience. After flicking through quite a few pages, I found the next page of writing about when Granddad went into the Imjin River.

*When I awoke, the dim light suggested a time just before dawn. The layered bracken had kept me relatively warm overnight and as I cautiously moved from my position, I realised it was too silent. There was no early morning bird song. Something was wrong. My brain told me to remain still. I took a deep, silent breath and listened carefully for sounds. The silence was broken by the sound of running feet and then the terrified scream of a female voice. I scrambled out of my hiding place, put on my still-soggy clothes and headed towards the continuing cries of fear.*

*Whilst keeping well out of sight, I saw a young woman of about 20 being chased by three young men in uniform, along the river bank on my side of the Imjin. My escape and evasion training made it clear that under no circumstances should I reveal myself to the local population and under no circumstances should I interfere with local disagreements between groups or individuals. So for the time being, I decided to observe the situation from a safe distance. The three men soon caught the young woman and roughly manhandled her back the way the chase had proceeded. I followed silently always keeping the trees between me and them.*

*Clearly, the men were North Korean soldiers but who was the young woman? After about half a mile along a well-worn single-file path, they left the trail and headed away from the river moving on to higher ground. I followed, careful not to close the distance or give my position away. The young woman seemed reconciled to being a captor and did not struggle. They topped a rise and disappeared down the other side. I would now need to be careful not to silhouette myself against the early morning skyline. To be absolutely certain of not being spotted, I crawled for about the last five yards before reaching the summit of the ridge. Then I carefully peered over the top. Below was a wooded valley and I just caught sight of the group disappearing from view. Would it be prudent not to become involved I wondered? Perhaps, if I rescued the young woman, she might be able to help me return to my unit or at least point me in the right direction. The decision had to be made quickly or I would lose them.*

*My instincts told me a life could be saved with my intervention so I moved carefully down the steep incline along the well-worn path. I felt very vulnerable to ambush so was extremely alert, glancing from left to right, forward and behind constantly for any sign of being compromised. The steep path eventually levelled out and I came to a settlement of sorts. There were four or five basic wooden huts built around a central point with the land cleared around them to give the defenders a clear line of vision. As I cautiously approached the small settlement remaining in deep cover, I saw two guards languorously patrolling the perimeter in a very casual manner; obviously not expecting any incursions into the area. Skirting the small hamlet, I wanted to establish an approach that would allow me to move in and out quickly without being observed.*

*The two guards always stopped to chat as they met each other on their rounds; even to the extent of lighting each other's cigarettes when the habit took them. This was clearly a weakness in the defence I could exploit if I so wished. Now where was the young woman being kept? I heard raised Korean voices coming from one of the crudely built huts. The sound of someone being slapped hard reverberated across the clearing and I assumed that it was the young woman being interrogated. I had a clear line of sight as I lay close to the boundary of the clearing. After plenty of shouting, and sounds of punching and kicking, the door to the hut was flung open and two men appeared dragging the semi-conscious young woman on the tips of her toes away from the interrogation room. Her face was battered and bloody. They took her to an area deep in early morning shadow. All I could hear was a wooden door being opened and a body being dropped, followed by the rasping turn of a key in a very rusty lock. I then considered what, if anything, I would do. Rescuing her from the locked enclosure did not present too much of a problem. However, getting away from there with possibly the young woman still unconscious might prove more challenging.*

*I waited until the guards met again and swiftly moved through the shadows until I was close to the cage the young woman was captive in. I became still and listened carefully to the sounds in the close vicinity. I could hear the guards speaking rather loudly, the snores from the soldiers asleep in the various huts and the groaning of the young woman. Now I have a very limited ability with the Korean language although the likelihood of a Korean understanding what a Welshman is saying is laughable. But anyway, I had to communicate with the girl and try to gain her confidence so that I could attempt to rescue her if she wanted to be rescued that is. So I started and said quietly, "Chingu" (friend): No response! Then rather clumsily: "Ban-gap sum-ni-da" (Nice to meet you). No response!*

*Desperation was beginning to set in and I was beginning to feel anxious about how long I had been by the cage so I decided to retreat back to the original laying up position. The guards were still chatting animatedly so I just sank back into a line-of-sight position. They were clearly confident that their encampment was in a safe position. They then carried on with their patrolling, still in a very casual, unaware way and eventually came back together and I slipped back to the cage. I said quietly: "Naneun Yeo get-tug-in-ida" (I am British). "Nae ileum-eun Johnny"(My name is Johnny).*

*With that, she groaned and turned towards me. She had beautiful jet-black eyes and then shocked me by saying, "Your Korean is crap," in an amazing unaccented American twang.*

*I replied ironically, "Kam-sa-ham-in-da"(Thank you). She smiled at that and I just said, "Shall we go now or would you prefer to stay?" And that is how I met Mi Yong! The lock on the cage did not take long to pick and we headed away from the scene without any difficulties. Mi Yong told me that she was a partisan fighter working against the North Koreans and Chinese. She led me away from the river going north saying that the destination she was heading for was 30km(approximately 18 miles) away. She said that we would be safe at the Kwanumsa Temple near Taehung Castle not too far from Kaesong. She felt it unwise and difficult for me to return to my unit; particularly when the North Koreans and Chinese were advancing through the large gaps left in the stretched UN defences.*

I did not attempt to search for the next instalment as my dad was standing in the doorway of my bedroom looking concerned.

# Chapter 5
# Home Truths

It had been over a week since Granddad Johnny's funeral and my dad told me that he could not delay telling my nan about Granddad's daughter Mul Yong so was going to visit her and would I like to go along with him. I agreed with some trepidation and thought to myself that it was going to be an awkward meeting. Questions whirred around my head. I must have looked concerned as my dad asked if I was alright. I nodded in affirmative unconvincingly. I felt anxious about what we were about to do to Nan. We were going to burst the bubble of their wonderful life together with a hurtful truth. He wasn't convinced by my response as he hugged me and said, "We're doing the right thing!" I nodded more positively as that's what I needed to hear and I think he needed it too!

As the journey from Hereford to Llanelli takes about two hours, Dad and I had plenty of time to chat about Granddad Johnny amongst other things. Now we live in the 'Munstone' area of Hereford which is north of the city. One of the big jokes about Hereford is that they built a bypass like other cities only it went straight through the town centre so traffic is appalling. Even more recently, the council have put in a link road at a cost of 15 million pounds with the aim of relieving traffic congestion on Aylestone Hill and Edgar Street. Many Herefordshire motorists would suggest that the attempt has failed miserably and made the situation even worse. However, I'm sure many towns and cities have similar traffic issues.

We reconciled ourselves to taking twenty-five minutes at least to get to the Tesco roundabout at Belmont so that Dad could fill up with petrol. I took the opportunity to ask Dad what he actually did at the 'foreign office'. He was taken aback by the question and hesitated to respond for so long that I had to ask him if he had heard my question in the first instance. Dad responded cautiously by saying, "I'm not supposed to tell anyone what I do because it is top secret. However, you are old enough I guess! Can I rely on your complete discretion not to divulge what I tell you to another living soul?" He asked very seriously.

I stated incredulously, "Not even Mum?"

"Oh, she already knows, of course!" My dad retorted.

I laughed nervously and whispered, "What's all the mystery?"

"First of all promise you won't tell anyone?"

"Okay, I promise!" I heard myself say.

He took a deep breath and said, "Well, I work for military intelligence. Specifically, MI6!"

I pondered and said in a disappointed tone, "So what! Why is that such a big secret?"

"Because it is a secret, covert, and government department!" Dad uttered this in an almost pleading voice.

"How did you become involved with this secret group? It definitely isn't in school career advice!" I fired back at him in a sarcastic way. Dad went on to say that he was recruited whilst doing his degree and then a master's degree in Arabic and Middle Eastern studies at King's College Cambridge. One of the lecturers had been involved when he was younger. I was a little dumbfounded by this and said, "You're kidding, right? Cambridge University is one of the top two universities in the country!"

Dad replied with a straight face, "Well, what can I say…I must be naturally talented. Not to be boastful but I was also a Cambridge full blue at football, rugby and hockey!"

I choked and retorted, "Well, I've got to admit, this family is red hot at hiding their talents from the world in general. You are turning into as much of a mystery as Granddad Johnny!"

He laughed rather curtly and stated, "That's probably why I've just told you about what I do."

"Give me an example of what MI6 operatives do?" I went on. "Are you like James Bond for instance? Licensed to kill or is that thrill?" I said, giving him a wink and a nudge.

Dad said earnestly, "Nothing so adventurous! I'm just an analyst who occasionally goes out into the field."

I suddenly had a thought. "Just before we get off the secret agent subject; I was doing some research about the SAS and they have a very mysterious E squadron. Do you know anything about them?"

"Ooh, that's interesting. You have been doing your research!" came his rather too-bland response. After that, he didn't seem to want to talk about it any further and as I was about to start pulling his leg about what he does, I thought it was time to let it go so we started discussing how 'he' was going to tell Nan about Mul Yong. We travelled on the 'heads of the valleys' road and as usual, it was misty, with clouds clinging to the hills and drizzling, driving rain.

When we arrived at Nan's house, she sat us in the lounge and made a cup of tea as she always did. The lounge isn't very big. As you walk from the kitchen, there is a large window directly in front of you and to the right a smaller window. There's a sofa along the back wall and two armchairs on either side which really are too big for the room's dimensions. The walls are covered with photographs of various family members and the one that always attracted my attention since childhood was one with Nan and Granddad on their wedding day. They looked so young and so in love. Nan looked so beautiful in her very ornate white dress with a beautiful headdress.

Granddad was in a brown suit with a white shirt and silk brown tie. He had a red rose in his jacket lapel and both of them were smiling naturally at each other. Of course, there were photos of me, Liam and Rhianna at various stages of childhood. There was a photo of Mum and Dad on their wedding day and a photo of Dad at his graduation ceremony wearing a gown and mortar board. That photo always inspires me to want to be a graduate myself! As Dad was sipping his tea from a proper cup and saucer; whenever my mum saw the tea set she gave an 'ooh isn't it lovely' coo of delight. Dad dunked a biscuit before asking casually if she had ever been given any information from Granddad Johnny about any previous love interests. She replied curiously, "Why do you ask?" That 'spooked' Dad.

Sorry, it just still makes me smile to myself. He obviously did not have a plan of approach as he clearly had not expected a direct question so I jumped in with one. "Nan, did you know Granddad had a large box in the attic which holds a lot of information about his life before he met you?"

"Well, Bach, he used to go up there occasionally and stay up there for a while. I thought he was checking the water level in the tank, but 'no' I didn't know he had anything up there," Nan responded in a puzzled tone. I explained that when she had given me the letter from Granddad on the day of the funeral, he had directed me to the box in the attic.

Then Dad thankfully chipped in and said, "Now, Mum, what I'm about to say will be very upsetting but you need to know." My nan looked perplexed but didn't respond. "Whilst in Korea, Dad had a romance with a North Korean lady called Mi Yong and they had a girl called 'Mul Yong'; if she is still alive she will be around sixty-six years old. The lady he had the child with was executed by the North Koreans as a spy. Dad tried to find his daughter but the situation with North Korea has made locating her fairly impossible. Obviously, this was quite some time before he met you."

"Oh dear," Nan said quietly and was silent for a long moment before saying, "you'll have to excuse me as I need to go outside for some time to ponder the information you've just given. Help yourselves to some lunch and I'll be back shortly."

When Nan came back in from the garden, it was clear that she had been crying. However, she did have a steely look in her eyes. "I don't pretend to understand why Johnny didn't tell me about his daughter or the girl's mother. Perhaps, he was embarrassed for any number of reasons, but I would have understood but he didn't give me the chance. I am deeply hurt by his lack of trust. After all, we had been married for fifty-four years and all that time he kept it secret. But Alan, I want you to do everything in your power to find, what is it you called her?"

"Mul Yong, Mam!" replied my dad sympathetically.

"Yes, do everything in your power to find Mul Yong; and just one more thing…I want to see the contents of Johnny's box and the 'black book' when I'm feeling more emotionally ready." At that point, Dad pulled out a large brown envelope and carefully took the contents out. As we had discussed previously, they were the 'gogok' jadeite pieces. Dad explained the history and that his dad, over the years had occasionally sold a piece to help finance their lives.

Nan looked taken aback by this and said in a rather frightened way, "Am I supposed to know how to go about selling these precious stones and negotiating the best price for these pieces? I must admit I don't feel competent or confident to do so!" Dad told her not to worry and that he would do some research and get back to her about the best way of dealing with the jadeite. Nan looked relieved, put the jadeite back in the envelope and gave it back to my dad, ending with a heavy sigh! With that, Nan carried on as if nothing had happened. It wasn't long before we left to return to Hereford. We were both thoughtful on the return journey. However, I did ask Dad about his childhood. At first, he wasn't particularly forthcoming so I questioned him about what schools he went to and this is what he said.

"We lived in Bryn Road, Upper Loughor until I was ten. Dad built the bungalow we lived in. It took him three years to build as he could only do it part-time as he was fully employed as a mechanic and of course, he ran a 'martial arts' school. My brother Tom is three years younger than me and we went to Upper Loughor Primary School. We moved to Bynea and I went to Bynea Primary School for my last year. Harry, who is eight years younger than me was just a toddler when we left

Loughor. I passed an exam called the 11+ which entitled me to go to Llanelli Boys' Grammar School. I was there from the age of eleven to eighteen. I was good at learning but I didn't like school. My parents bought me a bicycle for passing the eleven-plus and said that becoming a 'grammar school' boy would open lots of doors for me as far as future careers were concerned.

I was good at sport but looking back, 'socially awkward' and quite obstinate and stubborn. The grammar school was very keen on promoting rugby, which I was good at! However, because it was pushed so hard I became resentful and then favoured the 'round ball', football! Out of school, I joined a football team called Gorseinon Athletic. I was quite small for my age but terrier-like in the tackle, tactically aware and a good distributor of the ball. I remember playing in the cup final at Steboneath Park against a team called Trallwm Rangers. They had beaten us rather easily in the previous two league fixtures. The team were mainly Llanelli Grammar School Boys and I was told, at school, in no uncertain terms that they were going to absolutely thrash us in the cup final.

I am quite a driven, stubborn sort of individual and I saw their comments as fighting talk. I was determined to thwart their arrogance by doing everything in my power to stop them from defeating us in the final. The day of the final came. I remember being in the changing room with the team and giving a rousing speech as to why we would fight for every inch of turf on that pitch. I told them that we were going into battle and that our team would be the victors because we wanted the win more than them. I'm proud to say that we beat Trallwm 3-0! Mel and Dai our coaches couldn't believe it. They were delighted. I will always remember that day.

When I went to school on Monday, no one spoke to me. I couldn't help but chuckle to myself! But I did make a note to myself that poor sportsmanship should not be rewarded."

Dad talked about his time at university and we had a long talk about my ambitions in life. The time just flew by. I realised that I really liked my dad. Not just as a dad but as a friend.

That evening, I emailed Harry Thomas the first person to speak at Granddad's funeral, asking him to give me all he knew about Johnny.

This is his reply:

*Dear Kerry,*

*Tom Bonilla has been in touch with me and has filled me in on the information he has given you about Johnny. I came across your granddad quite a few times in my military career.*

*The first time I met him was during the Normandy landings. The 2nd Battalion of the Glosters was involved in the second landings on Gold Beach. There had been massive German resistance during the first landings and our forces had a great number of casualties. The resistance to the second wave of landings was not as great. Johnny was a member of Phantom F Squadron reconnaissance group which was the GHQ Liaison Regiment. They worked in small four-man patrols giving real-time information about the location/strength of enemy and ally troop movements. As you can imagine, it was a fairly dangerous job; more stealth than anything. He and his chums approached us after we had fought our way towards the Seine and gave us information about enemy strength and distribution of tanks, infantry and artillery. They were rewarded with a cup of tea. He spoke to me I suppose because he heard the Welsh lilt in my voice and asked where I was from. Well, I come from Neath originally and he said he knew right away I was from there. Even though it's only eight miles from Llanelli, the accent is very different.*

*Then I saw him again at a river crossing near Arnhem. We both exchanged pleasantries over a cup of tea and some hot food before he was on his way again. I heard through different sources that his Phantom unit started working with SAS headquarters in different theatres of the war still doing what they do best; infiltration, exfiltration, and real-time communication, always deep behind enemy lines. Rumour had it that they were so sought after that US forces used their expertise as well.*

*I also know that he was in Palestine in '47. I was quite surprised to see him appear as our intelligence officer in Korea. I was his company commander with the rank of captain. He informed me that he had been seconded from the $21^{st}$ (Rifles) Special Air Service and that he had passed the selection process in 1947. When he was reported Missing in Action during the skirmish at Gloster crossing on the Imjin River, I must admit I wasn't too concerned as he had proved time and time again previously that he was a resilient, courageous and indefatigable character who was pretty hard to bump off. Of course, I was right. Funnily enough, I didn't see him again until he rescued me from the same camp as Tom Bonilla.*

*I still have quite a few contacts in the army so I will approach a few others about him. In the meantime, would you be so kind as to take a photo of his war medals and email it to me? I can ascertain quite a lot from them and approach people accordingly. Hope this has been of assistance. Oh, by the way, I organised the honour guard at the funeral. They were current SAS soldiers; I believe from 'B' Squadron, his old squadron. It was the least I could do for such a brave man. Also, I meant to tell you that there was someone in the congregation during the funeral that was out of place. I don't know if you saw the elderly lady accompanied by two young men in the chapel and at the graveside. Her face looked oddly familiar. Any idea who she is?*

*Kind regards*
*Harry*

So, I wasn't the only one who had noticed the elderly lady and the two fit young men! I was becoming more and more curious.

I was beginning to feel that Granddad's history was coming together quite nicely without having to go on the internet and pay money to acquire information about my family's past. The 'Phantom' regiment's most famous soldier was 'David Niven' who, for those who don't know, was a famous actor who unofficially played James Bond in the film Casino Royale. It seemed to me a most obvious transition from regular soldier to 'Special Forces' for Granddad Johnny. Over the next few days, I continued to peruse the black book and over some page-turning, found the following narrative.

# Chapter 6
# Kwanumsa Temple

*The terrain en route to Kwanumsa Temple was fairly hilly and heavily wooded. Mi Yong, although not willing to admit it, was suffering badly from the beating she had suffered at the hands of the North Korean officer and his subordinates. She had been captured after blowing up a bridge on a main route used by Chinese and North Korean forces. They were trying to extract information about the whereabouts of the partisan's base and what other plans they had for disruption. Her earlier attempt at escape having failed she had resigned herself to being tortured to death. She was determined though not to give any information away. She felt that they would have killed her if that information wasn't forthcoming quickly. We had to stop quite often and there were times on the march that I had to support her bodily.*

*Nevertheless, I was impressed by her fortitude, sheer stubbornness and good sense of humour. We drank from mountain streams of crystal clear water which sustained our thirst but did little to sate our need for food. The air became colder as we moved up higher and even though the walking was arduous we shivered with the cold. During our breaks from the trail, Mi Yong, eventually, volunteered information about herself as long as I did the same. Surprisingly, she told me that she was a member of the Korean royal family and had spent much of her childhood in Tokyo. The family had been usurped from their position during the Japanese occupation of the Korean Peninsula during the Sino-Japanese War. The royal family had been assimilated into the Japanese royal family and in the main been reduced to positions of minor nobility.*

*In our conversations, it was clear that she was very well-educated and had learned English from an American tutor. She had returned to her country of birth at the age of 18 in August 1950 when the war broke out between the North and the South. She stated that she detested communism and wanted to return the country to a united Korea. I told her a little about myself but in truth, I was more cautious than perhaps I should have been. She told me that our destination, the Kwanumsa Temple, was one of two within the Taehung Castle fortifications; the walls of which, although mainly ruined and covered in vegetation ran for ten kilometres, incorporating the mountains of Chonma and Songgo.*

*We moved as quickly as possible through the landscape both motivated by the hope of food in our stomachs. After approximately eight hours of difficult terrain, we moved down into a valley where the temple was situated. We were carefully watched by a number of sentries who had not challenged us during the descent, obviously recognising Mi Yong. We had arrived at one of the partisan strongholds. A seven-tiered pagoda stood at the centre of the settlement. It was spectacular and seemed to be the main communication point. The carvings on the doors were truly magnificent and Mi Yong whilst running her sinuous hands over the carved reliefs told me that it was thought that a twelve-year-old boy carpenter had created the beautiful scenes. Apparently, the boy's mother had been taken ill whilst he was working at the temple and his superiors had declined his request to go and visit. Subsequently, the mother had died and the boy blamed himself for the tragedy and cut his carving hand off. Soon after, he disappeared. On a partially carved entrance door, there was a depiction of a young boy with a hand missing riding a white tiger up to heaven.*

*After eating and drinking our fill, Mi Yong and I were examined by a partisan doctor. Her injuries were treated and I had my wound dressed. We then both went our separate ways to rest up after our arduous escape. After some rest, I met Mi Yong's father and some brothers working with the partisans. Mi Yong explained who I was and that I had rescued her from certain death. They were all relieved and welcomed me warmly. Also, I met an American captain by the name of Saul Benjamin who was inserted with the partisans as a liaison officer directing operations and calling in air and artillery support.*

*Funnily enough, he worked for the 8240th unit; the US special operations unit I was due to be assigned to after having been in the country for six months. He relayed my arrival to headquarters and after some gentle interrogation, I was deemed to be who I said I was. Captain Benjamin seemed impressed by my military service and eventually, I was accepted into the group. I led small units of partisan fighters in attacking communication lines, blowing up bridges and road crossings, derailing trains carrying supplies and military armament. We were also used to call in air attacks on trains and vehicle convoys. The white tigers became a thorn in the side of the Chinese/Korean military to such an extent that rewards would be given to anyone who had information about our whereabouts.*

*My approach was always to move away from large enemy forces if they threatened our group because, after all, we were a guerrilla force, not an army. Mi Yong and I became very close during this time. Her father gave me a bagful of gogok as thanks for saving her life. He said that they were jadeite pieces from the tomb of a great Korean emperor, an earlier ancestor and that they were worth a small fortune. Quite honestly, neither he nor his sons were enamoured by our growing closeness and did everything they could to keep us apart. I trained the partisans to work in small four-man teams. I taught them tactical movement in hostile territory which involved them learning about night/day navigation whilst travelling through different terrain. Dealing with geographical/man-made obstacles like river crossings and highways was particularly important to avoid detection and contact.*

*Each man learned how to patrol taking into account team positions and covering arcs of fire. They learned how to track, counter track and prepare ambushes. Contact drills were practised using different scenarios and enemy strength. A team member was trained to use radiotelegraphy and became capable of sending and receiving Morse Code at speeds of between 12 and 18 words per minute whilst also being able to service the equipment in the field and maintain radio security. Covert surveillance and reconnaissance skills were essential elements of what we were tasked to do so that was drilled into my four-man teams.*

*The four-man teams also amalgamated to make larger forces and also trained for these formations. Intelligence gathering I felt was our primary role and that information would then be relayed to headquarters for them to assess and determine their course of action. Captain Benjamin felt that I was too cautious in my approach to this form of warfare. He had a more gung-ho attitude that created friction between us which we tried hard not to overspill into our mission planning. Nevertheless, there were times when I felt that we were placed in extremely dangerous situations where we came close to being captured or killed. I trained the partisans in hand-to-hand combat which they found hilariously funny but were nonetheless respectful.*

*I asked Mi Yong why they were amused and she explained that they were already being trained in self-defence by a man named Myung-Duk-Choi who had been an unarmed combat instructor at the royal court. He was with them at the temple and she offered to introduce him to me. After the evening meal, she took me to a large space inside the pagoda and there I met the man himself. He was in his seventies and of small stature. However, he exuded an energy or presence that belied his physical diminutiveness. He sparred with Mi Yong and his movements were like watching swirling liquid. His stance was low and he twisted and turned without any jerkiness as if his mind was one with his body. He was lightning fast, his balance almost balletic in form; every motion was smooth and seemingly effortless. Power was used sparingly and he tended not to respond to force but to move with it and use it against his opponent. I was fascinated and awed at the same time. I had thought my own prowess in self-defence was quite advanced until I saw a master in action. I* would not have stood a chance against Mi Yong's instructor. I went away feeling rather dejected and inadequate.

The next morning at breakfast, I asked Mi Yong if Myung-Duk would consider instructing me. Mi Yong pondered the request thoughtfully and then responded by saying it was unlikely that he would as I was a foreigner or oegug-in and he was very much a traditionalist. Nevertheless, she would ask on my behalf. She returned later with a rather crest-fallen expression and confirmed his refusal. I asked her if it would be alright if I observed him teaching others and she went to ask the master. This he would accept. So, whenever I was free from military activity, I went to observe him instructing members of the partisan fighting group. He taught them how to kick and punch whilst stationary and on the move; joint locks, throwing and strangling techniques were used whilst in closer proximity to an opponent. His instruction seemed very naturalistic and intuitive. He encouraged them to fight to their physical and athletic strengths whilst always reminding them that force should not be met with force but that the force of their opponent could be deflected and used against them.

Ironically, this was my martial policy for guerrilla tactics against the enemy. I asked Mi Yong if she would interpret for me if I engaged in a conversation with Myung-Duk about the philosophy of his martial arts instruction. She agreed and so began a dialogue with the great man that I found very instructive and I believe he found a little interesting. Eventually, after probably discussing my leadership and strategy skills with partisan members, he agreed to tutor me. In the short time, I spent with this grand master, I learned enough to instruct others and so began my intense relationship with all forms of Korean martial arts.

*My relationship with Mi Yong became more intimate much to the chagrin of her father and brothers. There were even some threatening remarks from one of her siblings that I found very disturbing considering that we relied on each other whilst on active service. I would have to watch my back. My relationship with Benjamin, although in public cordial, was deteriorating rapidly. He wanted our contacts with the enemy to be in far larger numbers to make more of an impact. I'm sure he was trying to curry favour with the powers that be to gain promotion and further his standing in the US military. I was of the opinion that morale would take a mighty fall if a mission went badly wrong and we would then lose the support of the partisans. Anyway, before the situation came to a head, I was called to the US army headquarters in Tokyo to report on my thoughts as to how well the partisans were supporting the war effort. I did not feel that this was a coincidence and convinced myself that Benjamin had been talking up the chain of command. Perhaps, my time with the 8240th Special Operations group was coming to an end.*

Granddad's writing began to get bigger and less well-formed at this point in the narration. He must have been tired. The piece of writing just came to an end. I decided that a bit of research into the deposed Korean Royal family would be in order so I asked my younger sister Rhianna to help out with this. That evening, I had to train at Usk in preparation for the upcoming tournament. I would not be teaching the youngsters, but sparring with the senior Dan grades and practising my forms. Interestingly, Dad had been given some information from a colleague from the 'foreign office' about someone called Yi Mul Yong! He wasn't 100% certain that it was 'our' relative but he was making further enquiries. From what Dad had learned, Korean names are arranged by surname or clan name first and then first names follow.

A child by that name had left South Korea in March 1955 destined for adoption in Texas! If she was born around the beginning of 1952 then by 1955, she would be around three, which didn't fit in with the supposition that the child had been taken to the north with relatives at her birth. If only Granddad had told my dad much sooner, he might have been reunited with her before his death. Dad's friend promised to continue looking for Mul Yong. I went with Dad to the Usk dojang and for three hours, I sparred with a succession of very accomplished 'Dan' grades that all had different styles of fighting. I felt that I held my own, just! I also worked hard on my 'forms'.

I tried to make a habit of reading some of Granddad's writing each day and came across this passage whilst page-turning:

*At one point, we were tasked with a mission to check the wreckage of a downed F86 F Sabre jet fighter severely damaged in a dog fight in an area towards the Chinese border called Mig Alley. We were tasked to make sure that the enemy wouldn't be able to use the cutting-edge technology inside the plane in any way. The pilot, who was credited with 14 MIG kills had ejected over the sea and was being picked up by a rescue helicopter. I had a gut feeling that this mission would be more dangerous than anticipated. I suppose I was feeling vulnerable because of the hostility being shown to me by Mi Yong's father and brothers.*

*In retrospect, I firmly believe that Mi Yong's father and brothers had decided that my relationship with her had to end and that they had determined that the only way was to get rid of me. Tellingly, they were away from camp on another reconnaissance mission when the directive came in. Mi Yong was away from camp collecting intel from the local population on the whereabouts of varying Chinese forces. So, our eight-man team moved to check out the wreckage. The coordinates we were given meant that the plane had come down to the west of our position; approximately twenty miles from our camp. Now whenever we had to travel openly through the countryside, we used typical North Korean mechanised transport with all the correct markings and flags. The partisans wore correct and authentic North Korean military uniforms; there were even some Chinese soldiers in our group that I had transferred from Malaya.*

*To add further authenticity to this mission, I would wear a Russian Air Force uniform to give credence to the cover story that we were going to capture a downed American pilot and analyse the technology of his plane. A colleague by the name of Xing Li was the person assuming the leadership role in our mission group if challenged by the enemy. He had previously been an officer in the Chinese Army before moving to Malaya; he had agreed to the secondment because he knew me well from our time together at a Jungle Training Centre.*

*The journey to the crash site was mainly on roads of varying quality and whilst there were sightings of Chinese and North Korean forces, we were not challenged in any way. However, the terrain became too difficult for our transport so we had to camouflage the vehicles and continue on by foot. The last known whereabouts coordinates suggested that we were five miles approximately from the site. Over the type of terrain we were travelling through, it would take around two hours of cautious movement. Our eight-man team moved in single file ten yards apart, the lead scout alert to signs of an enemy in the area, looking down and off into the distance constantly, whilst also turning to observe those behind him; then I as team leader was next, taking compass bearings and assessing less obvious routes of travel.*

*The terrain reminded me of the hills in the Brecon Beacons. Scrubland dotted with clumps of bushes and grasses with the occasional hardy sapling tree. Whenever the lead scout looked back, I would hand gesture the route we would take. The third man was the flank scout whose job was to provide arcs of fire to the front of the team leader and to the left flank. He was also involved with me in tactical navigation. The fourth man covered the right flank and was expected to keep a pace count until we reached our next navigation reference point. The fifth man was our radio operator, the sixth our medic and the seventh man my assistant team leader, Xing Li who was the Chinese guy I had brought over from Malaya. His role was to keep a careful note of the team's position and route whilst covering the rear scout whose job was to remove signs of the passing of our group.*

*Wherever possible, we travelled in cover, walked in each other's footprints, along rocky ground, using gullies and dried stream beds, never silhouetting against the horizon. The rear scout and second in command obliterated any sign of our passing whilst the lead scout moved us swiftly through the terrain. We were travelling at an acceptable pace of 15 minutes a mile. Suddenly the lead scout stopped, raised his hand with fingers splayed and crouched and tilted his head to listen and look. We all froze and stilled ourselves. There clearly was danger ahead. We all with one mind moved into deeper cover with the lead scout coming back to explain what had spooked him; whilst everyone else moved into defensive positions. He explained that a smell had alarmed him. A smell of stale body odour amongst all the natural smells had set his senses twitching. We examined the map to verify where we were exactly and established that we were approaching a river and that the land fell away quite steeply down to the water. He felt that there was definite human activity ahead and that we should consider the worst-case scenario of an ambush being set.*

*Crossing points would have to be examined as we could not avoid the river. I decided that scouting the river for crossings was the best approach. So, I sent the lead scout on a wide right loop away from where the perceived ambush might occur. The rear scout went on a wide left loop whilst the rest of us lay quietly in deep cover. I noted their time of departure and lay back to wait as patiently as I could. After an hour, I was beginning to be concerned. However, soon after, the rear scout returned and reported that he had scouted downriver and that there was no sign of any human activity. He also stated that crossing would be very dangerous as the water was deep and rapid. A little while later, the lead scout reappeared and said that there was a ford across the river but that it was held by at least 20 North Korean soldiers who were well hidden. He had travelled further upstream but felt that the flow of water would be too great for us to cross. He had then moved downstream cautiously and observed the group guarding the ford.*

*As a group, we discussed our next course of action. Our route had been decided back at base with the need for speed determining the most direct avenue of approach. We wondered if the ambush was set specifically for us. Could someone have supplied the enemy with the route information that quickly? The organisation and efficiency needed for the ambush to be set did not seem credible to me. The only other conclusion was that the mission had been compromised. I ordered our radio operator to contact our base by heavily encrypted Morse Code relaying the situation and asking to further verify the mission objective. This message came back:*

*Contact made with headquarters. No knowledge of downed aircraft! Mission compromised. Abort.*

*After some discussion, it was decided that we would withdraw the way we had come. So in routine formation, we headed back. The lead scout started working further forward remaining just in sight of the group. The rear scout did the same so that we would have a good warning of an enemy attack from behind. The lead scout came haring back with the news that a large force was moving towards us at the front. The rear scout also came running with the news that there was an enemy force coming at us from behind. We had been spotted!*

Granddad Johnny only ever seemed to have time to write one page at a time. Come to think of it, if what Nan had said about him going into the attic to check the water tank was the only time he wrote, then he obviously would not want to be up there too long or Nan's interest would be aroused. He always broke off and continued at a later date on a new page somewhere else in the book. Very confusing! He sometimes even wrote the book the wrong way up. You'd flick through and find pages upside down if that makes any sense.

That evening, I found a scrap of paper on the pillow in my bedroom laying out the information Rhianna had said she would obtain about the Korean royal family. She clearly did not like to waste words and her writing style was succinct but typically, she had done what she had said she would do.

1. Joseon Dynasty, the ruling house of Korea was founded in 1392.
2. In 1894, because of the military threat from China and Japan, the Korean court declared itself an Empire.
3. King Gojong assumed the title 'Emperor' in an effort to place himself on the same level as the Chinese and Japanese Emperors.
4. This attempt failed because Korea no longer had the military backing of either China or Russia because Japan militarily dominated the two countries.
5. The dynasty was deposed in 1919 when the Japanese annexed the country.
6. Japan's agents assassinated Gojong's consort Queen Min and then forced Gojong to abdicate.
7. Korea became a protectorate and then a colony of Japan.
8. After Japan was defeated in the Second World War, Korea was liberated from Japanese rule in 1945.
9. After the war, the Korean royalty was not reinstated because the President of Korea, Syngman Rhee, felt that they would undermine his authority as the new

republic's founding father. The royal family's properties and other wealth were seized.
10. There are a number of members of the royal family living in areas of the USA.
11. Yi Seok, born in 1941 is regarded as the nominal Emperor of Korea. He lives in South Korea, although he has spent much of his life in the USA. His father Yi Kang was the second son of Emperor Gojong. Yi Seok is regarded as the 'Singing Prince' as he had some success in the music industry in South Korea and with Koreans living in the USA. However, he is searching for a successor as his health has diminished.
12. The male members of the Korean royal family generally had wives and even concubines. Some of the male heirs had many children so unless we have Mi Yong's father's name, we cannot establish her lineage within the family.
13. Having examined the family tree, there is only one name that fits the time frame and that is Yi Jeon. His family name was Jonggil. He was an officer in the Japanese military during the Second World War. However, history records that he was prevented from returning to Korea after the Second World War and in 1947, Douglas MacArthur, as Supreme Commander for the Allied Powers (SCAP) removed his royal status. He had two boys and a girl by his first marriage. The two males are named Yi Chun and Yi Ki. The girl is not named.

I pondered the information Rhianna had given me and wondered if there was anyone in the Korean Royal family who knew that Mi Yong had given birth to a child before her death. As I settled down to sleep, I reminded myself to search for the rest of the account I had just been reading.

# Chapter 7
# Adrift in a Sea of Uncertainty

A few days later, Dad's colleague got in touch with him with more information about Mul Yong. Contact had been made with representatives of the Colt adoption agency who had been instrumental in finding adoptive parents for Korean War orphans. There had been a Mul Yong taken from South Korea to America in 1955. She was approximately three years old. Specifically, she had been placed with adoptive parents in the state of Texas—in the city of Houston. The timelines, as I've previously stated did not coincide with the information that Granddad Johnny had spoken about in his letter to me; and the assumption that the baby had been taken north by relatives was concerning. Dad had been asked by the colleague how he intended to proceed with the information. We 'FaceTimed' Nan and asked her what she thought. Not to disappoint either side or get hopes up, she felt that some tentative information should be exchanged.

Nan asked me if there was anything in what Granddad Johnny had written that might help us verify that this Mul Yong was Granddad's long-lost daughter. I had a moment to think and Granddad's words came to mind about how a fellow partisan had described the baby. I said, "Mul Yong was born with very blue eyes and she will have a dimpled chin!" We all agreed that it would be unlikely that Mul Yong had any first-hand information about her parentage so we couldn't count on her for accurate information. Dad informed his colleague that he would like to make contact with Mul Yong in Houston.

Dad was given the Colt adoption agency to contact, which he did, and passed on his email details in the hope that Mul Yong would make contact. The agency had also informed him that it was up to her whether that would happen. They would simply inform Mul Yong that a British man was searching for a mixed-race child born during the Korean War who may be related to him and would she describe herself and tell him what she knew of her story.

A week or so later, Dad had this email:

*Dear Alan,*

*My name is Mul Yong. At least, I've been told by others that it is my name. I believe I was born in the month of March 1952. I do not have a birthday so have adopted the 1st day of March so that my birthday can be celebrated. I am sixty-six years of age and have never married or had children. Being discarded at birth leaves a residual feeling that is hard to escape and has probably affected and determined my life choices. They say I am of mixed race or biracial, the result of a Korean woman and a white man. My skin is white in complexion, but I have very black hair (streaked now with grey) and very green eyes. I am quite tall and considered slim. My face shape is a mix of Asian and European. I have a round face with a dimple on my chin and my eyes have an occidental look, giving away my Korean ancestry. People call us American Asians.*

*When I reached the age of majority, the adoption agency sent me all the information they had on me. I was found in a wicker basket at the entrance to an abandoned Buddhist temple. Apparently, above me on a door entrance to a pagoda was a carved scene of a boy riding a white tiger. An old woman found me and took me to the local priest who sent me on to the nearest orphanage. At that time, many Korean children became orphans because of the fighting. The old woman must have given quite a bit of detail about where she found me; perhaps with the idea that someone would be looking for me. In the basket was a note written in Korean which stated that my name was Mul Yong, that my mother had been killed and that my father was a Westerner; whereabouts unknown, nationality—probably American.*

*Because of my lack of racial purity, the extended family had abandoned me. I was placed in an orphanage near the Imjin River. The people at the adoption agency told me that I was taken from Seoul, South Korea to America at the age of three. I have no memories of my early years in Korea. I have lived my adopted life in the United States—not always happily. I was adopted by a very religious couple who live on the outskirts of the city of Houston. I lived with them from the age of three until I was eighteen. They were too strict and bullied me into religion. They did not show me any love or really care for me. They wore my adoption as a badge of their goodness in front of others rather than any thought of nurture. They did provide me, however, with security, comfort, food and financial support which I have to be grateful for. I left as soon as I lawfully could. I did not do well in school and left full-time education very poorly qualified.*

*In school, I was good at sports. I had excellent coordination and was particularly adept at martial arts, gymnastics, archery and team sports. In fact, I was so good at archery that I represented the USA at the Olympic Games in Montreal in 1976. I didn't gain a medal but the experience was simply amazing and confidence lifting. To be honest, sports kept me interested in life. As a child going to church seemed to be the only thing I was ever allowed to do. Then one day, I was walking to church and noticed some kids, in what I could only describe as black pyjamas, talking excitedly and heading to a large building. Curious, I followed. That day changed my life. They were going to a martial arts class. So, at the age of 10, I started training in martial arts much to the dismay of my adoptive parents.*

*The owner of the dojang allowed me to train for free which I will always be eternally grateful for. I have been practising for over 56 years. I am the owner/instructor of three schools and am a grand master of Korean martial arts. My greatest regret is I never found out who my parents were! My life in America has never made me feel fulfilled. I speak with an American accent but don't feel American. I remain an unanchored soul, tortured by my unknown past floating on a sea of constant uncertainty. However, hope remains in my heart. I have proven on many occasions to be a resilient individual and one day, I will learn about my history! I have visited South Korea, even been to the places mentioned in the file the agency has on me, but that land does not hold any connection for me. Places don't make connections. It's people that do! So, I remain in a twilight world not fitting into the West or the East. But I survive! Do not feel sorry for me. It is a life that I have chosen for myself. I am told by the agency that you are searching for a relative. Good luck and I hope you find him or her. You now have my school's email address, so if you require anything further from me then feel free to make contact.*

*Regards*
*Mul Yong*

When my dad showed me this email, I had to read it a number of times. It was so sad and yet I was filled with hope. No wonder, Granddad had not been able to find Mul Yong, he had been looking in the wrong place. This person could really be my great-aunt! Dimpled chin and green eyes, but the clincher for me was where she was found! She was a 'Grandmaster' of Korean martial arts. She was even an Olympian. Amazing! Granddad Johnny would have been so proud! Dad contacted Nan and read the email to her. He explained why I was so excited. We composed Dad's reply to Mul Yong very carefully indeed.

*Dear Mul Yong,*

*My name is Alan Morgan. I am fifty-four years of age and come from Hereford, England; although I originally come from a town in Wales called Llanelli. We have recently been given a book of memories written by my father Johnny Morgan who also came from Llanelli. In the book, he relates some of his wartime experiences in Korea. Whilst working with anti-communist partisans behind enemy lines, he had a relationship with a lady by the name of Mi Yong. Her family name was Yi. She became pregnant and whilst Johnny was reporting on the partisan successes in Tokyo, she gave birth to a baby girl.*

*The baby was born in March 1952. The girl was given the name Mul Yong which is Water Dragon in English. The couple intended to marry when he returned from Japan. Distressingly, whilst he was away, the Chinese/North Korean army took the partisan stronghold; reputedly, Mi Yong was captured and executed. It was thought that the baby was taken North with the Yi clan. Johnny reluctantly went back to the UK towards the end of the war. He tried through various contacts with the partisans and with US army connections to find where his daughter had been taken. Unfortunately, the relationship with North Korea meant that all of his investigations as to her whereabouts came to nothing.*

*Dad sadly died recently and whilst going through a box of his belongings, we found a reference to his daughter. She was born on the grounds of the Kwanumsa Buddhist temple near Kaesong in what is now North Korea. In my father's writing about his time at the temple, he makes reference to a carving of a boy with a missing hand riding on a white tiger up to heaven. Also, my dad had green eyes and a dimpled chin. Johnny Morgan, my dad, rescued Mi Yong from interrogation and certain death by the Chinese near the Imjin River.*

*Mul Yong, I believe you are who we are looking for. I am your half-brother! I have two younger brothers. I have three children. Kerry, my eldest child, has been studying Dad's writing and is very excited about this wonderful news. I know this information will knock you sideways emotionally and you may even be sceptical about what you have just heard. I will send you some pertinent extracts from my dad's writing so that you can come to terms with what I am saying to you.*

*In addition, you need to know some unusual similarities between the life you chose and the way we have lived. Johnny Morgan was also a grandmaster of Korean martial arts. He also had martial arts schools, two in fact. My brothers and I are now the instructors at the two schools since he passed away. Kerry, my daughter is training for her 3rd Dan. By all accounts, Mi Yong, your mother, was a serious exponent of Korean martial arts. What is more, Dad's writing informs the reader that she was a member of the Korean Royal family! Dad never said what day you were born in March 1952 but there is a strange irony here. The day you chose, the 1st of March, is called St David's Day in Wales. St David is the patron saint of Wales and the day is one of celebration and dressing up in costumes. We realise you may be uncertain about pursuing your connection with us so will wait to hear from you. I know this is too much to take in so I will conclude by saying, You have a family!*

*P.S. I will photocopy the appropriate passages from Dad's writing and attach them to this email.*

*Kind regards*
*Alan Morgan*


After reading the email numerous times, Dad and I decided to press the 'send' button! We both wondered how Mul Yong would handle this earth-shattering news! We reconciled ourselves to quite a long waiting time for a reply as the news would take some assimilating.

Surprisingly, a reply came the following morning. Dad thought that Houston was six hours behind the UK. So Mul Yong had written the email in the early hours. This is her reply:

*Dear Alan,*

*I have been reading the information you have sent me trying to take it all in. In fact, I have read it so many times I think I could recite it in my sleep. Talking about sleep, I haven't had any since receiving your email. Part of me wants to leap with joy and yet another part of me says, I should be cautious. I have cocooned my emotions for a very long time so that hurt cannot reach my inner being. I find the information you have sent compelling and I believe what you are saying is true. So, my father was called Johnny Morgan and my mother Mi Yong! I have the names of my parents at last. I am saddened that I never got to meet either of my parents. I knew as I grew older it was less likely that my father would still be alive.*

*Nevertheless, it would have been wonderful to meet him. May I ask you to send me some photographs of my father and if at all possible my mother? I always thought my father was American and now find that he was Welsh. I'm not even certain where Wales is! And you say, I have three half-brothers. Wow! If you don't mind, I would like to continue e-mailing you with any questions I have and also can you tell me about you and all the family—if you don't mind!*

When Mul Yong replied and asked for some photographs, I went to look in Granddad's box and started sorting through his collection. There were lots of photographs of men in army uniforms: in the desert, in the jungle, in urban and rural areas, alongside various vehicles, eating food.

I eventually came across a photograph of Granddad with a woman, an oriental woman—on the back in Granddad's writing was 'Mi Yong and me' May 1951. They gazed at each other lovingly with a building like a very ornate multi-layered birthday cake in the background. That must be the seven-tiered temple mentioned. They looked so very young. It was the only one in the hundreds he had. I went and found Dad to show him. I scanned the photo and Dad said that he would send it when he had a moment. He also said that work wanted him to go away for a time and would I take his place in communicating with Mul Yong. He was sorry to lay the responsibility at my door but he had to go. Obviously, I said, "Yes!"

So, I thought there's no time like the present:

*Hi Mul Yong,*

*I'm Kerry Morgan, Alan's daughter! I'm afraid Dad has had to go away on important business and he has asked me to fill you in on the family history and send photographs. I enclose a photograph of Mi Yong and Granddad Johnny, as well as a family photograph of Granddad's 90th birthday with all the close family. I have named them all and said what relation they are. Granddad had a friend by the name of Tom Bonilla who spoke a eulogy at his funeral; if you like, I can give you his email address as he was held prisoner in North Korea at the time and can give you further insight into your dad.*

I paused at that point because something was disturbing my train of thought.

I felt I knew Granddad's nature quite well and whilst asleep the previous night, I kept on going through in my mind all that I had read. Something was missing. It struck me like a bolt out of the blue. He would have written a letter to her in the hope that one day she would be found and have a chance to read it. It would also be well hidden as I sensed it would be a very personal and emotional correspondence, not for everyone to see I would presume. So I returned to the black book and scoured every page in search of the letter. I gently held the book by the spine and shook it. Nothing fell out! I decided to examine the box.

As I've said before, the box was very ornate. It had carvings of dragons and tigers in relief on the outside covered with a brown lacquer. On the inside, there were red dragons and white tigers embroidered onto a green satin background. I felt around the inner contours of the box and there was definitely a slight rise in the fabric where the wing of one of the dragons touched the corner of the box. I put two fingers carefully behind the fabric and gently closed two fingers around the raised area. It felt like folded paper and I lifted it from the confines and with bated breath unfolded it. It was a letter written in Granddad Johnny's neat cursive style.

*Dear Mul Yong,*

*My name is Johnny Morgan. I am your father. I write in the hope that one day you will find out about your parentage and come looking for me. I have put some information about my early life in an ornate box that I've asked my granddaughter Kerry to look after and to go further by telling my story. Please believe me when I say I love you with all my heart even though we have never met. I have tried so hard to trace your whereabouts in North Korea but to no avail. The people I used to work with have all tried their best to find you and I have even pressurised the US administration to negotiate with North Korea as to your whereabouts. Obviously, this has been unsuccessful.*

*I am dying. My heart is no longer strong and it won't be too long before it gives out. Oh, if only I could have met you and told you about your mother and how you were loved and are loved! Well, this letter will have to make up for a lifetime of not knowing!*

*Mi Yong, your mother, was a member of the Korean Royal family. The family were usurped during the Japanese occupation of the Korean Peninsula and were removed in the main to Tokyo where they held positions of minor nobility. Your mother was well-educated and besides Korean, she spoke English, with an American accent. She was beautiful, funny and a determined woman. Everyone loved her because she was kind, a loyal friend and could always be relied on to do the right thing no matter what.*

*We fell in love whilst working together against the communist forces in Korea. Her father and two brothers were also part of our combat group. They were not happy with our developing love for each other and did try hard to get me killed or at the least captured by the Chinese. Clearly, they failed. It was our intention to get married after the war had ended. We were ecstatic when Mi Yong became pregnant. Just before your birth, I had to report to my superiors in Tokyo on the success of the partisan operations. When I returned, I was informed that the partisan stronghold had been overrun and that Mi Yong had been executed as a traitor. I was also told that my daughter had been taken North with the Yi clan which I was relieved about.*

*Mul Yong, I hope that you have had a good life and oh, how I wish I could have been with you growing up. Every 15 March, I feel terribly sad thinking about what you are doing on your birthday. At Christmas, I think of all the presents I have missed giving you. I think about you getting married, having children and grandchildren. I think about what you look like as an adult. I have a wife who has been my partner for fifty-four years and I love her dearly. I have three boys, Alan, Tom and Harry. The three boys are married. I have seven grandchildren.*

*Being without you and not knowing what happened to you or where you are has been a constant source of torture for me. A part of me has been missing since I lost you and your mother. I have never given up hope though. However, as my time draws to an end, I must assume that this letter will be the only connection I can have with you! Mul Yong, we both chose your name as we met near the Imjin River and it flows through the valley of the Water Dragon. Mul Yong means Water Dragon.*

*I have always found speaking emotionally very difficult and tend to be a rather matter-of-fact sort of person so please forgive me if I appear lacking in that area. Mi Yong was at her most brilliant when working under extreme pressure. She kept a cool head under difficult circumstances and was always a strategic thinker. She was a team player and motivated others with her organisational skills; her tenacity to get a job done well and her personality shone through to such an extent that there was an aura about her that was comforting. Everyone who came into contact with her—loved her. Her instincts for survival were acute. When the partisan stronghold was overrun, her overriding concern would have been to get you to safety no matter what the cost to her would be. I still carry a feeling of terrible guilt for not being there when the attack happened. I've often wondered what Mi Yong did to secure your safety and even after many years of trying to find out, I could never glean the details of how you escaped the attack.*

*If you are as determined and as focused as your wonderful mother was and perhaps a little like me then you will have had a successful and meaningful life. I don't think I can say any more to you. I love you and will go to my grave thinking of what might have been if we had the chance to meet.*

*Bless you, my daughter.*
*Your loving father!*

Reading Granddad's words made me sob quietly to myself! So sad they did not get to meet. If only Granddad Johnny had shared this secret. I will, of course, scan the letter and send it to Mul Yong, although I better notify Dad of my discovery first, just in case there is something I have overlooked.

I returned to the email I had been preparing to send to Mul Yong and sent it asking her if she could send some photographs of herself so that I could show the rest of the family.

I contacted Dad by 'WhatsApp' and told him about the hidden letter that Granddad had left Mul Yong. He was a little busy attending to his work so would consider any difficulties that might arise. I then 'FaceTimed' my nan and with the exception of the hidden letter gave her an update on the communication going on with Mul Yong. She asked that when I next came to visit I bring Granddad Johnny's black book as she felt ready to read its contents. She also asked that Dad contact her to discuss a letter she had received from a storage company asking if Mr Morgan wanted to renew his annual storage agreement with them and if not he needed to remove all the contents from the storage unit.

It's quite telling that when I read the black book, I search out parts that I'm attracted to and as I learn more about Johnny Morgan's life, the details and more importantly, the context of what he is trying to say come through. I flicked through the pages once again and lo and behold I came across an inventory of items stored in the storage unit that Nan had just had a letter about. I'd probably flicked through before but never registered the significance. To say that it was a detailed inventory would be an understatement. Also, there seemed to be an extraordinary range of items—some of which were seriously large if as I scanned correctly they were full-scale. I got in touch with Nan and told her about the storage unit inventory. I read out some of the items and we both agreed that it would be best to wait for Dad to accompany her and that it was best to renew the lease for another year.

Later that day, I had a heart-rending email back from Mul Yong saying how much the letter from her father had upset her, but also that she now did feel that she had been loved by someone! Even though they had never met! She also had been given her true date of birth. She also sent through some photographs of herself. She was tall and slender with beautiful green eyes that seemed to have a vitality that twinkled with energy. She did have a dimpled chin like Granddad and Philip which did make me smile. She was a very beautiful woman who would be noticed as soon as she entered a room.

# Chapter 8
# Bad News

A week later, in the late afternoon, Mum had terrible news about Dad. She gathered the three of us together and told us that he was in Queen Elizabeth Hospital Birmingham having been 'medevacked' from wherever he had been. He had gunshot wounds and was in intensive care but in a stable condition. At this point, she had to tell the three of us what Dad actually did. Obviously, I knew, but Liam and Rhianna were gobsmacked and horrified. Mum phoned Nan and Dad's two brothers to break the news. After the difficult news had been passed on to close relatives, the three of us travelled up to the Queen Elizabeth Hospital. It would take approximately 1 hour 40 minutes and in that time, Mum faced a barrage of questions about Dad's occupation from Liam and Rhianna. I was asked by the two of them why I didn't have any questions and at that point, I had to reveal that I had stumbled across what Dad did whilst researching Granddad's mysterious life.

They even in a jokingly/sarcastic way asked Mum if she had any life-changing mysteries she wanted to share. She paused before saying, "I met your dad in Hereford as you know. I have never said in what capacity, or where exactly in Hereford we met. I suppose I should with all the revelations about your dad's life being revealed. Long before you were born, I enlisted in the army at the age of 21. It was 1989 I believe. As I had a 1st class honours degree in classics…"

I interrupted and asked, "Which university?" Mum smiled and said, "The best, of course, Magdalene College Oxford!"

I could not help but roll my eyes and say, "You cannot be serious, one parent attended Oxford and the other Cambridge. Unbelievable! No pressure on us then!" I said slightly exasperated.

Mum kept on grinning inanely and decided to continue. "I thought I would put it to good use by joining…the army! I know most people would see that as a foolish career move for an Oxford graduate, but I've always wanted to test and challenge myself and try things outside my comfort zone. Well, I certainly did that! I went into a Signals Regiment as a 2nd Lieutenant and for seven years, slogged really hard to reach captain. I then transferred to military intelligence and whilst based in Hereford, I met your father. I left the service in 2000, Kerry when I had you! If you have any questions about military intelligence, I can't answer them, so there!"

Liam was intrigued and asked a very interesting question. "Did Nan and Granddad Johnny know what you did and what Dad does, if that makes any sense?"

Mum hummed quietly to herself before saying, "I told them I was in the army and that I was in the Signals Regiment. After that, they didn't seem to ask again. As for your dad, he always maintained the story that he works for the 'Foreign Office'. Whether they believed him I really couldn't say." We chatted then about Dad's career, but I felt that Mum still wasn't telling us everything. We arrived around seven thirty and went to the reception area at the front of the hospital.

As soon as Mum gave Dad's name, a person was phoned and within moments, we were whisked away to a section of the hospital reserved for injured/wounded military personnel. We were escorted to a waiting room where we remained for half an hour. There were facilities available which allowed us to have hot drinks. Eventually, a middle-aged female doctor came into the room and explained what had happened to Dad. He had been shot in two places. One round had gone through the top of his left thigh and the other through the left shoulder quite high up. The lady doctor continued, explaining that the shoulder wound wasn't too serious as the projectile had passed straight through without thankfully damaging too much, although a great deal of blood had been lost.

However, the shot to the left thigh had damaged the left hip joint. They had operated on him and the damage had meant he needed a replacement hip. This they had done. He was in intensive care because his body needed to recover from the trauma caused by two wounds and of course the reconstructive surgery. He was heavily sedated and had a profusion of tubes in him, but we were welcome to see him although he would not be aware of us.

We were then taken through some doors guarded by two armed red-cap soldiers, then into a room where we were each asked to put on white overalls, face masks, visors, gloves and shoe covers. We were then accompanied down a long corridor and into another room where there were four sectioned-off areas each containing an occupied bed and an array of machines. At the entrance to each section sat a nurse on a high chair in front of what I can only describe as a lectern as if the person was about to make an important speech. However, it was noticeable that each nurse gave their whole attention to the patient in front of them; at times getting up and checking equipment and then making notes.

Dad was in what appeared to be a transparent gossamer shroud. He had tubes and bags hanging everywhere and he looked very pale. It was a very disconcerting scene and I felt like crying but instead bit hard into my bottom lip and kept a stern control over myself. We didn't stay there long as there was no point. We went back to the waiting room with the lady doctor who had greeted us. She explained that when they deemed him ready he would be transferred to a high-dependency ward and then further assessments would be made on his progress. Mum asked the doctor, who was the consultant surgeon who had operated on Dad, whether she should stay. The consultant said that there was little point as he would not be cognisant for quite a few days.

She stated that the hospital would keep us informed of his progress and would let us know when he was ready to have us visit. Mum put up some protest about this but between us all, we persuaded her that it was in everyone's best interest. We left the hospital in a very subdued manner and travelled home to Hereford. I phoned Nan on my mobile and updated her on Dad's condition. She said that she would come with us when the hospital said it was right for us to visit.

When we arrived back at our bungalow in Hereford, I sent an email to Mul Yong explaining that Dad had been injured and was in intensive care. I didn't go into detail as she had to take in an enormous amount of information recently as it was. She replied almost immediately stating how horrified she was and that she was sorry to hear such sad news. She also attached photographs of herself in various situations and at different ages. I could see aspects of Granddad Johnny's face and it was somewhat unnerving. I sent the attachments to my nan. She 'WhatsApped' me back pretty quickly saying how astonishing it was to see him in her face. In my email to Mul Yong, I explained that we were waiting for the hospital to inform us of Dad's progress and whether we could visit and I ended saying that I would keep her up to date with events. I contacted Dad's friend in Usk who ran the dojang when he was away and explained the situation. He was fine about standing in! I said that I would try to get down for a session as soon as I could.

Over the next few days, our anxiety about Dad grew. Mum contacted the hospital at the same time each day and got the same answer. No change. Then on the third day, the consultant rang and explained that Dad was awake for short periods but still very groggy. She felt that he would be able to see us the next weekend. Mum stated that she would stay in the accommodation building when we went up so that she could be there with him each day. We informed Nan and she said she would ask Uncle Harry to take her up.

The week went far too slowly. All we wanted to do was see him. Eventually, time did pass and on Saturday, we travelled to the Queen Elizabeth Hospital in Birmingham. Mum travelled up on her own and I drove with Liam my navigator and Rhianna the back seat driver. We were met by the female consultant we had seen before and a gentleman dressed in military uniform. The man took my mum to a side room and they had, what I can only describe as a heated argument. Mum came out very red-faced and with a very steely defiant expression. I asked casually about what the conversation was about but she brushed my concern away by saying she would explain at a more appropriate time. Nan and Uncle Harry joined us with the lady consultant explaining that Dad was making good progress. After getting out of bed, he had taken a few faltering steps supported by a pair of crutches. The pain management regime was effective but he pushed himself which meant that he tired quickly.

At that present time, he seemed fairly energetic so could see visitors. But only three at a time! Nan, Mum and I went in to see him first. He looked remarkably well for a man who had been shot twice and had only recently had a hip replacement. Nan and Mum sat on either side of him both holding his hands. I stood at the end of the bed quietly regarding the whole scene and not really listening to the conversation, just celebrating in my own mind that he would be alright. After a little while, I did hear Mum say in a rather too-loud whisper, "Where the hell have you been?"

My dad gave a reply that my mum was obviously very used to. He stated apologetically, "You know I can't tell you that!"

She retorted in a very fierce whisper, "Tell me or I'm off!"

With that, Dad gave a very long sigh and said quickly, "North Korea!"

I think we all thought and said, "What!" at the same time in tones of varying astonishment.

Dad looked around secretively and said, "This could take a little while as it is a complicated story." We were all ears.

"Well, the information we have gleaned about my dad's escapades in Korea got me thinking. I thought the situation warranted some further exploration. With the permission of the people I work for, I asked our analysts to ascertain for certain that Mi Yong had died in the Kwanumsa Temple attack. Philip was very helpful as he got some of his former associates in the CIA to also do some digging. After a great deal of research and greasing of many palms, they found evidence in the North Korean historical archives in a top-secret file that some prisoners had been taken from the site. Mi Yong was on the list and so was one of her brothers and also her father. However, even more astonishing, her father had a baby boy with him and it is thought to be Mi Yong's child!"

We all gawped at this revelation. I said plainly, "So, Mul Yong is not Granddad's child then?"

Dad nodded in the affirmative and carried on, "Yes, she is! Mi Yong had twins."

Well, the looks that we all gave beggared belief. Mum said, "Then why was Mul Yong left and the boy taken?" Dad took a long, deep breath and paused as if dragging the information from a drug-addled mind. "I've been told by Mi Yong that she was in another part of the stronghold when the attack came. She had left the children with the wife of her 'martial arts' instructor. After her capture, she was reunited with her father and her son at the internment camp. She had hoped that the baby girl would also be present, but that was obviously not the case. Her father had managed to rescue the boy but not the girl. Mi Yong questioned her father about what happened to Mul Yong and all he could say was that the boy was more important and he couldn't carry both of them. I could hazard a number of guesses as to why the boy was taken and the girl left.

Korea was and is a very traditional society. Boys are regarded more highly than girls. The children were illegitimate, which even in our country was frowned upon. So in Korea, it would have been a major issue. Generally, families in Korea sent the boys to school and the girls stayed at home learning how to be good homemakers. Yes, very discriminatory and sexist but that is how it was then. Another contributing factor may have been that the boy simply looked more Korean than the girl. Anyway, the MI6 analysts continued to look into Mi Yong and with a great deal of subterfuge established that she was placed in a political dissident's camp. She remained incarcerated there until the war fizzled out. Her father had some political and financial influence so basically, they bought their freedom.

However, they were not allowed to leave the country. Her father died quite a number of years ago and she has remained under house arrest until recently. In a good turn of fortune, they lived in the suburbs of the city of Kaesong which is near the demilitarised zone that separates North from South; ironically, only a few miles from where they were taken prisoners at Kwanumsa Temple; all those years ago. I decided to have a word with Mi Yong as they do not have access to mobile phones or the internet. So with the help of some North and South Koreans, plus the Americans, I crossed into North Korea and visited her in Kaesong. Obviously, this was done in the utmost of secrecy, with the help coming from inside and outside the country. I went in as a member of a British film crew given permission to film a wildlife documentary showing how the demilitarised zone had become a haven for rarer animal and bird species because of the lack of a human presence.

Whilst filming, I managed to break away from the film crew unnoticed. I was accompanied by two Koreans, both the grandsons of former members of the 'donkey4' group that my dad worked with during his secret missions behind enemy lines. Without those two young men, I don't think I would have got back."

Mum interjected at that point and said, "How did you get shot—twice?"

"Well…everything was going really well." My mum rolled her eyes. "I'd had the chat and we were heading back through the demilitarised zone and got within 50 metres of a crossing point when we stumbled upon a patrol of North Koreans who decided to shoot instead of asking questions. It was a close call but we managed to get back over the border to the south without me losing consciousness or too much blood. I suppose I may have been carried at some point but hey, let's not dwell on that. Once in the hands of the South Korean authorities, I was relatively safe, thanks once again to Philip smoothing the way through his contacts. He was there in South Korea coordinating the whole operation."

He stopped talking at that point and stared expectantly at my mum. She stated sarcastically, "I'm sure that you have left out much more than you have said, but as you are not fully recovered, I won't vent too much anger yet. You bloody fool!" My nan just kept on holding his hand trying not to smirk. Undoubtedly, he had left a great deal out!

I said in an enquiring tone, "What shall I tell Mul Yong when I email her?"

Dad's rather too-quick response was, "Just tell her—I'm on the road to recovery!"

Not too long after, we left Dad's bedside, for the other three to have some time with Dad. We went for some food and a hot drink. Mum had made arrangements to stay at the hospital whilst Dad was recuperating so went to reception to get the keys to the accommodation. We all went with her to see where she would be staying. Her room was clean and cheerfully decorated. It even had a television. There was a communal kitchen and laundry room. Whilst we were getting our bearings, Mum had a conversation with a lady in the laundry room who had been using the accommodation for three months. Her husband was recovering from a heart transplant.

We agreed with Mum to keep in touch by 'WhatsApp' video and then went our separate ways. The three of us got back to Hereford at quite a late hour. I just could not settle to sleep so I pulled the black book out and searched for the continuation of the account I had been reading last. As I've said previously, it's not just a question of flicking through from front to back; some pages were upside down! Frustrating at times and quite eccentric! But I was becoming familiar with the way Granddad did things. After a bit of searching, I did find the next part.

*When a small force is faced with a much larger force to your front and back—what should you do? Well, it's quite simple. Split up and skedaddle. Standard operating procedures had been drilled into this group and without any fuss, the group divided into pairs and moved away to left and right. Our rendezvous point would be back at the camouflaged vehicles.*

*I travelled with our radio operator. He made carrying quite a heavy load look easy and there were times I struggled to keep up with him. We stayed in as much cover as we could. We heard sounds of gunfire indicating that some of the pairs in our group had made contact with the enemy. We all knew not to take direct routes back to the rendezvous point. We took the approach of hide then move, hide then move, making absolutely certain our movements were not seen. We crouched, crawled and slithered our way from danger. It was exhausting. But the alternative did not bear thinking about. If caught, we would be interrogated for the whereabouts of the rendezvous point and subsequently our base of operations, then once the information had been obtained—shot!*

*The route that we took back to the RP was circuitous; we avoided open spaces and kept in cover. We reached our destination at twilight. We watched and waited. Nature always gave clues to the presence of man. Yet, there was the evening birdsong that occurred all over the world. A good sign! Still, we waited and watched. Darkness spread like a blanket over the area. There was some ambient light from a waxing gibbous moon. Had any of the other pairs made it back I wondered?*

*I decided to move things along by cupping my hands and making the sound of an owl. I moved, and made the sound again! To our left, there came a similar sound. Then it was repeated at a different location. I gestured to the radio operator to stay where he was and that I would head towards one of the camouflaged vehicles. I pulled my commando knife from its sheath and crouched and crawled towards our vehicles. I sensed, more than saw someone to my left, crouching by the right front wheel tyre of the vehicle I had been driving. I made a noise to make him aware of my presence and moved towards him.*

*In the moonlight, I recognised him as my second in command, Xing Li the Chinese guy I had worked in Malaya* with. We spoke very quietly. He informed me that he had the rear scout with him watching for the incoming enemy. He felt they had avoided being followed, but he was fairly sure that at least one pair had either been captured or killed. We considered our options. We could wait for the others to come in. The four of us could leave in one vehicle, leaving the other vehicle for the late-comers. After a brief discussion, we agreed to wait for a little while longer so each of us headed back to our partner's laying up position. We waited, shivering in the moonlit cold, as clouds obstructed the light of the moon.

After a reasonable amount of time, I decided that we needed to move. So I moved forward overtly so the other pair were not in any doubt as to my intentions. I moved to the vehicle we were going to leave for the others and checked there wasn't anything inside that would give us away if the enemy located the transport. The four of us climbed into the vehicle after removing the camouflage netting and the foliage used to break up any discernible silhouette. As the vehicle was on a slope, I released the handbrake and we quietly rolled down the hill before I put the gear-stick into second and released the clutch without revving too heavily on the accelerator pedal. We did not use the headlights and moved through the landscape hopefully without drawing attention to ourselves. I hoped that the others would make it...

The attack was unforeseen. I drove through a rocky ford and the road then began to rise steeply. I was in a low gear when all hell let loose. It was a long time ago so I don't remember specifics but the front windscreen must have been shattered by the gunfire as I remember wiping away shards of glass and blood from my face. It was difficult to see because the blood was streaming into my eyes. Xing Li, the front-seat *passenger had been hit in the upper body and was screaming in agony. Behind him, the radio operator was unmoving and lolled with gaping wide eyes. A round had hit him in the middle of the chest. Dead! I gripped the steering wheel even tighter. The world zoomed into just me driving.*

*I tuned everything out and drove to survive. I kept wiping blood from my eyes whilst steering the vehicle determinedly away from the ambush. We did manage to get away and made it back to base. Xing Li recovered slowly from his wound. The other four from our party did not make it. They were hunted down and shot. Five out of eight fatalities was a difficult statistic for me, as the leader of the group. It took quite some time to process. Informing relatives of the death of a loved one was and is the hardest thing of all.*

Once again, Granddad Johnny came close to a life-or-death situation. I don't know if I could see myself in such difficult scenarios. I think I would panic and then that would be it. Perhaps, keeping a cool head, in difficult circumstances, is the key to survival!

The next morning, I emailed Mul Yong and informed her that my dad was making progress. She replied quite soon after saying she was relieved for us and to keep her informed. She also said that she would be away for a few days judging a mixed martial arts competition in Mexico City. She called it the Pan American Games.

Mum 'FaceTimed' me and we chatted for quite some time. I asked her about the uniformed man she was arguing with before we went in to see Dad. She said that she knew him from her time in military intelligence. The argument arose because she was annoyed with the intelligence service for allowing Dad to go off on a 'hare-brained', Mum's words, 'adventure'; with little backup and poor preparation. She also added the bombshell, "Your father brought Mi Yong out of North Korea with him. She is being questioned by South Korean officials to ascertain her allegiances and why she wanted to leave after all this time."

I interrupted and asked: "What about Mul Yong's twin brother? Where is he?"

"Dad was fairly vague about what he knew but did say that he was a high-up official in the North Korean government," my mum replied.

We chatted for some time, mainly about Dad's condition and Mum's experiences in the accommodation and around the hospital. She was very complimentary about the care Dad was having and raved about the hospital staff, particularly the Filipino nursing staff based in intensive care. The conversation was coming to an end but I had to ask, "Who is going to tell Mul Yong that she has a twin brother?"

Mum stated, "We need your father to consider that question!"

That evening, I contacted Tom Bonilla by 'FaceTime' as he had become somewhat of a good friend to me. I explained about my dad and the little adventure he had been on. I updated him on all we knew about Mul Yong. He wondered about the twin brother as Tom felt that someone so high up in the North Korean government could be a dangerous factor or on a more positive note a good ally. I wondered what Dad knew that he wasn't telling us.

Mum continued to update us each day on Dad's progress. He was clearly getting stronger as he was now taking on flights of stairs with his crutches. He found the effort tiring but it was a good sign. The gunshot wounds were healing nicely and Mum thought that he would be cleared to leave in about a week.

I kept Nan informed. In fact, I kept everyone informed. Sixth Form College resumed in my life. I walk to college each day from the Munstone area which is approximately a mile. I had to prepare for my 'A' levels in English, RE and PE. On Wednesday evenings and Saturday mornings, I attended the 'dojang' in Usk. So, life was pretty full on! Liam was in the first year of sixth form and Rhianna was in her last year at high school getting ready for GCSEs. Oh, and the three of us shared the house-cleaning, food preparation and the washing and ironing in a civilised and cooperative manner; for most of the time. It seemed that we each enjoyed a particular discipline.

Rhianna was brilliant at the washing and ironing. Liam enjoyed cleaning and organising the three of us with the necessary finances to get us through each day. How absurd! Who'd have thought it? My forte seemed to be cooking the evening meal, then washing and wiping up. We muddled along quite happily. We tried our best to be there for each other as Mum was being for Dad. It was the least we could do!

Mum brought Dad home on a Saturday afternoon. She helped him out of the car with the three of us standing and staring then clapping with delight. He looked a little pale. He gritted his teeth. A sure sign that he was finding the whole ordeal painful! We all sat together that evening watching the usual rubbish on TV and were just so glad that we were once again back together. Dad asked me how it was going at the Usk dojang. I told him that his assistant sensei was coping really well. He then asked me about communications with Mul Yong. I reported that she was up to date with his road to recovery but that she did not as yet know that her mother was alive and that she had a twin brother who was also alive and a bigwig in the North Korean government. He felt that a few more days not knowing would be fine. He would tell her when he felt up to it.

I told him about the storage unit inventory. He thought it would be best if he had a look at it before his mum visited—just in case there was something there that might upset her. That would also have to wait a little while as he needed to deal with his own recovery first.

# Chapter 9
# New Beginnings

I went to bed feeling very happy that my parents were home. I perused the 'black book' for where I had left off the last time and for the life of me, I could not find the continuation page. But I did find an account that interested me.

*When I left the army at the start of the Summer of 1965, I had a difficult time adapting to civilian life. I missed the camaraderie most certainly, and whilst married life was enjoyable and becoming a parent exciting, I did yearn to challenge myself physically and mentally again. After all, it had been the only employment I knew. Working as a mechanic was interesting and the martial arts evening classes were popular. However, I did miss the risk-taking and the adrenaline rush that adventure brought. When I left the army, I was obliged to go on the reserve list. As I had been with the regiment, my placement was with the 21st SAS (Artist Rifles); basically a return to my roots!*

*I was approached by the commanding officer to do a job that was described as off the books. They needed my expertise in hostage negotiation or possible rescue as my reputation for rescue since the Korean War, amongst military people in the know, had apparently become legendary.*

*The person kidnapped was a female member of the British Royal Family. The kidnapping had taken place whilst she and her retinue were holidaying on the island of Bali, Indonesia. A team of experts would meet me in Brunei at the Jungle Warfare Training School at Seria. The Sultan of Brunei had been informed of the kidnapping and had offered the British Royal Family any support he could give. Interestingly, the school in Brunei was relatively new with the original school being in Johore, Malaysia. I had been an instructor there in the late 1940s. As the most senior ranker, being a major, I would command the group. The directive was to get the female royal out unharmed by whatever means. Paying the ransom was preferred but there was to be no shilly-shallying with the kidnappers. If they played ball, that was fine! If not, then I was to do whatever was necessary to get the female back unharmed.*

*She had been taken from a private villa under the noses of her bodyguards. She had been missing for two days. The ransom demand had been delivered to the British Consulate in Denpasar, the capital of Bali. The kidnappers were a faction within a communist terrorist group that had been creating conflict in the region for some time. They wanted 2 million American dollars for the return of the Royal family member. The consulate had bought us time by informing the terrorist group that bringing together such a large sum of money would take at least five days. The kidnappers seemed satisfied with the reason for any delay. I was to travel to Brize Norton and board the Sultan of Brunei's private jet. The hostage situation was to remain secret.*

*So I told my wife Mildred that I had to go away on exercise and would return within a fortnight. She was surprised at the short notice. As I was self-employed, Mil volunteered to contact my customers and explain that I would be away for a little while. I drove to Brize Norton and took the Sultan's private jet. We re-fuelled in Dubai and then travelled to Brunei. I was fast-tracked through customs and picked up by a black limousine with a rather smartly dressed chauffeur taking my luggage and opening the car door for me. With re-fuelling, I had been in transit for seventeen hours. However, the private jet was lavish in its facilities and I was able to sleep comfortably for eight hours, so I was reasonably fresh when I arrived at the Jungle Warfare School.*

*The team I would work with were already there. I was pleased to meet my old comrade Xing Li, the Chinese soldier who had been my second in command in Korea. He had been severely wounded during an ambush attack and it had taken quite some time for him to recover. He had joined the British Secret Intelligence Service (MI6) at the conclusion of the Korean conflict. I explained to the team that the prime directive was to simply exchange the female royal for the money. Once the location for the exchange was established then a team would reconnoitre the area and take up covering positions in the event of treachery. The kidnappers were informed that the money had arrived by the British Consulate Attaché and asked how they wanted to proceed.*

*I was not happy with this approach as it put us in the position of a subordinate doing as you are ordered. The kidnappers wanted the money to be placed in a given location and then the royal would be released. I didn't agree. If they wanted the money, then they would do it face to face. They could choose the venue for the exchange but it would have to be a face-to-face in open ground. One vehicle from each party would enter the open ground. I would bring the money. Two people from the kidnappers could bring the royal' In my communication with the terrorists, I further explained that as long as they were only interested in the money then everything would be fine. There would be no further reaction. There was quite a deal of attempted manoeuvring by the terrorists but eventually, they agreed. A venue and time was given by them. Just a window of 24 hours to get my team in place!*

*0600hrs the exchange would take place outside a Hindu cave temple near the town of Bedulu, which is about an hour north of Denpasar, the capital of Bali. We flew from Brunei to Denpasar Airport on the Sultan's private jet. It took approximately two hours. We went through the airport without any security intervention, picked up local guides and went to reconnoitre the exchange point. We reconvened and established our plan of action. I had four army snipers in the team and they were detailed in taking high ground with a clear view of the exchange site. They were arranged around the steep valley leading into the cave temple site and told to wait for orders. Each sniper wore a Ghyllie suit which is an amazing piece of kit that provides camouflage that is virtually impossible to spot. Xing Li would coordinate communications whilst I would drop off the money and pick up the royal. Any funny business would not end well for the terrorists. I arrived in a battered old American army jeep thirty minutes before the agreed time. I had agreed to communicate with the snipers by using hand signals. So, I knew every move I made would be watched carefully by at least one sniper whilst the others constantly traversed the area watching for impending danger.*

*The snipers had radio communication with each other and with Xing Li who would coordinate any action necessary.*

*At the allocated time, a grey vehicle entered the steep tree-lined valley. The vehicle stopped a hundred yards from my position. I got out of my vehicle and collected the bag containing the money from the boot. I stood by the driver's side door to observe what was going on with the grey vehicle. No movement. I put the bag of money on the bonnet of the jeep and pulled out 40 bundles of American dollars whilst still facing the grey vehicle. No movement. I randomly chose bundles of money and flicked through the wads to show that the notes were genuine. I gestured with my right index finger in pointing away and to motion that it was time for the exchange. A guy in the front passenger side got out and carefully checked for signs of anyone else being present. I reloaded the bag with the wads of money I had put out on display and walked as casually as I could manage to about halfway between the two vehicles and stopped. I dropped the bag onto the ground and stood expectantly.*

*The right-side back door opened and a rather burly man climbed out, turned and grabbed for the person who was clearly the royal. She was gagged and bound and her brown hair was extremely dishevelled and her goggling eyes were wild with fear. On further inspection, her clothes seemed to be in good order, although she didn't have any footwear. She was dragged by the man towards me. I remained still but vigilant. In that frozen moment, we all heard an unexpected noise. We turned in the direction of the noise. Clearly, from the expression on the burly man's face, he was not expecting any outside intervention and I most certainly wasn't. A large* open-topped truck, crowded with soldiers was coming down the hill. I said quickly, "What's going on?"

He replied in a heavily accented voice, "I don't know! It has nothing to do with us!"

He released the girl, took the money and ran for his vehicle. I put my arm around the young woman, led her back to my vehicle and gently guided her into the back left-hand side seat whilst releasing her bonds and pointing to a bottle of water on the back seat. She sighed gratefully whilst pulling the dirty gag from her face. The grey vehicle sped away in the opposite direction of the truck, wheels spinning and dust flying. There was little point in me getting into the vehicle as the truck had neared to an extent that I could not get away. I turned and watched as the soldiers piled out of the truck whilst a small, dapperly dressed little man walked cockily towards me. He said, "You are under arrest."

I said, "What for?"

"You are a foreign agent working without authority in my land," he said with a beaming grin.

"I beg your pardon? I'm here on a sightseeing visit," I replied nonchalantly.

"Then why do you have a tied and bound young woman in the back of your vehicle if you are just sightseeing?" He retorted in an even more annoying manner.

"I just parked here to go into the Elephant Cave when a car came to a screaming halt and without so much as a by your leave, discharged that young lady and skidded off at great speed. What was I supposed to do? Leave her on the ground and continue with my sightseeing?"

At that, the little man seemed a little perplexed. "Let us speak with the young lady to establish the facts then shall we," *was his challenging reply. With that, I returned to the vehicle and helpfully removed the young lady from the back seat. I looked at her expectantly, as did the little man. She did not disappoint.*

*"I was walking down the street in Ubud, near where I was staying when a car pulled up and a man grabbed me and bundled me into the back. They put a hood over my head and have been keeping me like this for some days. I'm just a tourist. It must be a case of mistaken identity. They must have confused me with someone of importance! Please take me back to the villa I was staying at as my friends will be so worried," the young lady responded, in a very convincing way.*

*The little man said, "I will need to verify your identity. What is your name? And where are you staying?"*

*"My passport is back at the villa. I am Rose Scott. The villa is in the grounds of Ubud Palace." The little man raised his eyebrows at the mention of Ubud Palace. But the young lady carried on regardless and said, "Can I be taken home by this gallant gentleman now, pretty please! You, of course, can follow in your dusty truck full of sweaty soldiers as my protection." With that, she fluttered her eyelashes, smiled and proceeded to head for the front passenger side of my vehicle. I turned to follow and heard the little man whisper to himself in heavily accented English, "That didn't go as planned." I smiled and walked back to the jeep.*

*I took the royal home, followed by the truckful of soldiers. In my rear-view mirror, I could see the little man gesticulating and ranting at the driver. He wasn't a happy chappy! Before leaving the site, I had used the radio in the car to tell Xing Li to stand down. During the journey, Rose Scott wasn't particularly chatty although seemed to be relieved that she had been rescued. She did ask me my name and thanked me most profusely for what I had done. I explained that it wasn't just me who had been involved in the rescue and that a large team of people had been involved in the exchange and more pertinently a great deal of money had been given for her safe return. She asked how much she was worth. I told her and she was taken aback before saying that she was going to be more careful in future and not put her own safety entirely into the hands of others.*

*We got to the palace, which was guarded by Presidential guards; the royal got out saying thank you as if I had just given her a lift from the supermarket and disappeared into the grounds of the palace. In my rear-view mirror, I noticed the little man approach the palace guards and in no uncertain terms being turned away from access. I even think he stamped his feet with rage. It was a rather peculiar affair all in all. I returned home and continued with my life.*

*A little while later, I received an award, much to my surprise. It was a secret award.*

How extraordinary! The rescue of a royal! Just like Granddad Johnny to always understate events!

A few days later, Dad emailed Mul Yong and asked if she would be willing to have a 'FaceTime' call with him. She replied that she would be happy to do so! Dad told us all that he was going to tell Mul Yong about all that had happened in North Korea. Whilst he knew we would all like to meet and greet her, it might be best to leave it for a later time. What he was going to tell her would be too overwhelming as it was!

When he came out of the study where he had gone to make the 'FaceTime' call, he looked thoughtful. I asked how it had gone so he told me. Mul Yong listened carefully to the information Dad had given her and then proceeded to ask the questions anyone would under the circumstances. Dad gave her all the information he could. Mi Yong was being questioned by the South Korean authorities; although a British representative was 'smoothing' the process. Dad felt that it wouldn't be too long before she would be released to travel anywhere she pleased. There was however the complication of obtaining a passport. He felt that the British government could also help with that.

Furthermore, Philip, with his contacts could also be of assistance. After all, she hadn't done anything wrong. In fact, she had aided the South Korean and American cause all those years ago and should be seen as a heroine. Obviously, Mul Yong was more than interested in her twin brother and Dad had told her that her brother's name was Yi Cheondung Yong (Thunder Dragon). Yes, he was a high-up official in the North Korean government. In fact, he had become their foreign affairs minister. He tried to influence Kim-Jong Un to have better and closer relations with South Korea and the wider world. Dad said that he seemed to be a good guy with good intentions. He had met him briefly whilst visiting and subsequently extracting Mi Yong from North Korea. In fact, Dad's visit and removal of Mi Yong had been a collaboration between the South Korean, British and American governments and Cheondung Yong. His mother was losing her eyesight and needed specialist treatment that was unavailable in North Korea. She would be taken to London after her interrogation by the South Korean Government and have a 'cornea' replacement procedure. It seemed the case of 'you scratch my back…'

Cheondung Yong would be grateful for the medical intervention and be cooperative enough to keep British and American intelligence informed of the goings on in the North Korean government. As you can imagine, Dad informed us, Mul Yong, became very agitated in her excitement at the news. She asked Dad to keep her informed about her mother and brother. She was desperate obviously to meet her closest family; people she had never thought existed. She also told Dad that she had been e-mailing Tom Bonilla and he had told her as much as he could about Granddad Johnny. It had given her great satisfaction to gain further insight into her father's life. She was also going to email Harry Thomas and chat with him about her father.

I reminded Dad about the storage unit in Llanelli and that Nan wanted to read the black book for herself. So we made arrangements to go and have a look at the unit and deliver the black book and I also decided to take the 'red dragons and white tigers box' and give it to her. We would go without Nan to the storage unit in the first instance. As Dad said, "It would be an idea to just make certain that there wasn't anything there that would upset her in any way." We contacted the owner of the unit with a time we wanted to visit. He said he would have a spare key ready for us. We would go on a Saturday morning as funnily enough everybody wanted to come. "To see Nan," they said, but I knew that they really wanted to see what Granddad had been storing all these years.

The excitement in the car Saturday morning was palpable. Mum drove as Dad was still using a walking stick and wasn't fit enough to drive. It was as if we were going on a treasure hunt. I hoped they wouldn't be disappointed. Having seen the inventory I knew they wouldn't be! That is if I had read the contents correctly!

Hereford traffic has a way of cooling excitement when you want to get somewhere quickly. From the BMW garage, passing St Francis Xavier's school and down College Hill took forever. Getting onto Edgar Street and passing the New Market development an age. By the time we were at the Belmont roundabout, half an hour had passed. Once we passed Tesco Belmont roundabout, we were positively flying. For once travelling along the 'heads of the valley' was sunshine instead of rain. Auguring a wonderful day perhaps!

We stopped with Nan for lunch. I gave her the black book and the box. It was like giving your children away. She commented that we all seemed very excited and excitable. Dad just told her we were pleased to be all out together for a change and of course, we were pleased to be visiting her. Patience is a wonderful trait as long as you are not in a hurry. There that's a quote from me! Dad did smile a lot and winked at all of us in turn. It was as if he was delaying departure deliberately to challenge the esteemed virtue of patience. Fidgeting, even by Mum became very noticeable to me.

Eventually, Dad relented and said that we had better be on our way. He gave Nan a kiss and hug. The rest of us kissed and hugged Nan and yes, we were on our way to the storage unit. We parked the car; Dad went to the office to fetch the key whilst we all milled about. Unit 24 was our destination. Well, I couldn't wait to see their faces. Dad and I had some idea at least what we would see. However, even our pre-knowledge had not prepared us for what we saw as we entered the unit. Astonishing is an over-used word but in this case, it was truly that. The storage unit was big. In fact, I don't know how best to describe how big it was except to tell you about the contents. I got the hand-written inventory out and asked them all if they wanted me to be their guide for the afternoon. So, we will start with the biggest stuff which is placed centrally in the unit and work our way from the centre outwards to the sides. Everyone looked gobsmacked as it was like walking into a military museum.

"This is a Willy's Jeep (M38A1) with a Browning and Vickers machine gun mounted centrally in front of the driver and front passenger; on the front left and rear left bumper is an identification symbol with green top and blue bottom square with 41 in black paint which represents the reconnaissance regiment. On the right-side front/back bumper is a black square with a white triangle signifying the 1st infantry division."

As I finished the description, Rhianna and Liam climbed into the vehicle and basically acted like a pair of school kids touching everything and pretending to fire the machine gun. Dad and Mum started to walk over to the other large vehicle so I rushed over to continue my next commentary.

"This vehicle is called the 'Pink Panther'. It is a variant of the Land Rover Defender110 series and has served the SAS since the early 1960s. It has a spare wheel mounted over the front bumper, no doors, as you can see, and an overall pink colour that allows the vehicle to blend into the pink haze often met in desert conditions. 'The Pinky' has a long wheelbase for a greater payload-carrying capability. The vehicle has two long-range self-sealing fuel tanks situated on either side of the rear gunner's small seat. There is a four-speed gearbox. The chassis has been adapted to provide suitable suspension in desert conditions. As you can see, there are spotlights mounted front and rear. The tyres are adapted for the desert. There is a sun compass and sand ladders.

There are various compartments that hold shovels, rifles, grenades, camouflage nets, storage for bergens and jerry cans for fuel and water. Smoke dischargers are fitted with two on the front bumper and two on the rear superstructure. The vehicle has a three-man crew. The armaments are impressive with two general-purpose machine guns mounted between the driver and passenger at the front and one at the rear that the third crew member fires. In Granddad's inventory notes, he mentions that the Pink Panther has every piece of equipment that it should have in place and that it took him quite some time and a lot of searching for authentic parts. Nevertheless, all his hard work has paid off with a vehicle of great beauty."

My brother Liam must have heard the last sentence as he shouted sarcastically, "Only because it's your favourite colour!"

I, of course, ignored him and carried on with my commentary but in a more aloof tone.

"This is an amphibious jeep called the Ford GPA GAZ 46 MAV 4x4 vehicle, which I'm sure military vehicle geeks would be very interested in. It is Russian-made and entered service in the 1950s. Only 654 were produced and this version apparently is very rare. Granddad Johnny says in his notes that it is road and waterworthy."

I said more to myself than anyone else, "This would be like being in a sweet shop for some military buffs!"

Well, at this point Mum and Dad climbed in and sat in the back of the vehicle. Rhianna and Liam waited for Mum and Dad to vacate the vehicle and did their touching-everything bit again. I moved to the rear wall and started examining a motorbike which I must admit was rather beautiful.

"This is a 'Royal Enfield Constellation' in pristine condition. This must be the bike Granddad and Nanny had the accident on. It has a red petrol tank with the word 'Constellation' in gold with gold stars at each end of the word. The seat is of black, glossy leather with lots of chrome in a highly polished condition.

On the saddle, there is a presentation box and inside it is a medal. It is a British Empire Medal. There is a letter from Queen Elizabeth II thanking Granddad Johnny for rescuing a member of the royal family from a hostage situation. Because of the sensitivity of the situation and the importance of the hostage, the award was given secretly and no mention of it has ever appeared in the press. There is a citation and letters of thanks from the Queen and the 'royal person'."

The whole family came over to have a look at the medal and read the letters and the citation.

Whilst they were doing that, I continued my commentary, more for my own interest than anyone else's!

"Here are three motorbikes—Matchless G3/L (lightweight). It is in camouflage green and has 'teledraulic forks', whatever that means. This is a 998cc 'Vincent Black Lightning' in mint condition. There were only 31 built and it was the fastest bike in the world in 1948. The third bike is a 'Matisse Desert Racer' in green with a British flag. It was made famous by somebody called Steve McQueen."

With that Liam and Dad smirked at each other. Liam said incredulously, "You don't know who that is? The Great Escape!"

I looked at him nonplussed and in an irritated way. I replied, "I'm not really into Macho role models!"

"He was a film star of the 50s to 70s and a keen motorcycle race competitor and racing driver. And yes, he was a real macho guy that men and women admired," responded my annoying little brother.

We were all blown away by the superb condition of all the vehicles and wondered how they were looking so good. We all then went to look at different things that interested us.

On my wandering, I saw a beret with a cap badge with side views of the Roman gods Mars and Minerva. There were many works of art depicting Second World War Scenes.

There were numerous statues of military men. Quite a few of them had parachutes strapped to their backs. There was a vintage record player with old vinyl 33 1/3 records: Music by Mario Lanza, Enrico Caruso and many others. In one area, there were dress uniforms of different regiments of the British Army. I don't have any knowledge about the uniforms of the British Army, but I did recognise the flying daggers of the SAS. There was a free-standing glass display case securely locked that held various hand-guns. Each pistol had a name tag stating the name of the weapon, the maker, how many rounds it fired and a little bit of history about the maker. There were wall-mounted cabinets that held very impressive rifles and machine guns. These also were labelled with the same formatted information as the pistols.

In one area nearer to the door, there were various forms of machinery for the repair and renovation of motor cars and motorbikes. There was a sea kayak and a river kayak with paddles, life jackets and helmets. There was a deep sea diving suit with modern and less so Sub-aqua gear with air tanks.

From the ceiling, there was an open parachute displayed and on a large wooden table, there were photograph albums of when Granddad Johnny was a young man, mainly sporting teams he played in with an assortment of family photos of his parents, and his siblings. There was also another 'black book' which I leafed through and it was arranged in the same higgledy-piggledy way as the one I had just handed over to Nan.

Then there was a knock on the unit door and a man stepped inside. We were surprised, but he wasn't. "You must be sensei Johnny's family," he said. "My name is Danny Butcher and I've wanted to give my condolences to you but I felt embarrassed."

I asked, "Why ever would you be embarrassed?"

His response took us all by surprise. "I was one of the boys that tried to beat Johnny up in 2004." We were taken aback by this. He explained that when they had been sent to Swansea prison, Johnny had visited each of them and forgave them for their attack on him. He had even given each of them his address and telephone number so that, if they wanted, they could get in touch with him after they got out. He had promised that if they did, he would help them in any way he could. The other two had laughed. He had not been so certain so he had given Granddad Johnny a telephone call and Granddad had kept his promise. Granddad had given him a piece of advice that he took to heart. *People talk about being on the right path or the wrong path. Always remember that you can get off the path and start your journey again.*

Granddad had found him a job at the garage he had worked at as a mechanic when he had left the army and they had given Danny an apprenticeship to train as a mechanic himself. He had also started going to the 'dojang' in Llanelli and was training for his 1st Dan. Danny said that Granddad had been instrumental in helping him turn his life around. He sorely missed Granddad Johnny. What is more, he was the one who had been keeping the storage unit in such fine shape. He visited every week and was collating all the pieces in there. We were all very impressed by this. Dad asked him if he would keep on doing his weekly visit and offered to pay Danny for his time. Danny said that it was a privilege to enter the storage unit and get to be with all the objects that Granddad had held so dear. He would not accept any payment!

He also added that whilst collating the items in there, he had done some research on the values of the motorbikes and the three military vehicles. He said that the 'Vincent Black Lightning' in particular, was, in his opinion, worth £750,000 if not more, as it was so rare and sought after. We were all astonished by this. The amphibious vehicle, Danny reckoned, was worth £70,000. The Willy's Jeep, £15,000. The Pink Panther, because it had every piece of equipment that it should, he felt was worth at least £65,000. The 'Matchless' G3/L, £4500. Royal Enfield, £7,500. Matisse Desert Racer, £11,500. A grand total of £923,500.

If what he said was true, then this collection that Granddad Johnny had built up over the years was worth an absolute fortune. I suppose, when Nan sees it, she will have to make up her mind about what to do with it. From what Granddad had said about the Gogok jadeite pieces, they were also worth a great deal of money and there were still 12 left. Dad and Mum looked very thoughtful with regard to what Danny had said about the value of the items in the unit. Nan would have to visit the storage unit 'pretty sharpish' as we now had a 'security issue' Dad said. He would get his brothers to set up a rota so that there was now someone there all the time until Nan had had a look and decided what to do with the collection. He would also ask his brothers Tom and Harry to take Nan for a visit to the storage unit as soon as possible. I wondered what Nan would do about all the items in the unit.

We travelled home to Hereford and whilst we were all fairly cheerful, there was that feeling that the 'storage unit' held a connection with Granddad's history that would be hard to let go! I'm pretty sure my brother Liam went to sleep that night dreaming only of those beautiful motorbikes!

On Sunday afternoon, Nan FaceTimed Dad and explained that his brothers had taken her to the storage unit that morning. She asked him about what she should do with the contents of the storage. She had already spoken to his brothers individually. She also explained that she and Granddad had joint wills. If he went first, she would inherit everything and vice-versa and in the event of both of them dying, the three boys would have equal shares. Nan and Dad agreed that really personal belongings like photographs, letters and medals should be kept as they meant something to the living. It was agreed that a specialist London auction house would be contacted by Dad as he had a friend who was quite high up in the organisation and would ask him to value the contents of the storage unit. Nan had already asked his two brothers if there was 'a small something' that they would want from the unit to remember their dad by. She also asked Dad. After some consideration, he said, "Could I have the 21st Artist rifle beret?"

Dad kept in touch with his brothers about the storage unit security and invited his friend from the auction house to visit the unit to value its contents. The man got back in touch with Dad who conveyed the valuations to Nan and what percentage the auction house would charge. The first auction would be of the motorbikes and military vehicles. The rest of the contents of the storage unit would be auctioned at a later date. They also talked about something called 'Capital Gains tax'. After some back-and-forth communication, everything was agreed and the auction house was given permission to take the items away; which was a great relief for my uncles! The auction would take place in a month's time.

Events began to accelerate. Dad was informed by SIS (Special Intelligence Service) that Mi Yong had been released by the South Korean Intelligence Services and the British Embassy in Seoul was arranging for her to travel by plane to Heathrow. The passport issue had been dealt with and she had been given South Korean citizenship. Dad was to pick her up and as he was still incapacitated as far as driving was concerned would have a driver for as long as he needed. He would take her to the private hospital in London for the 'cornea' replacement operation. He would remain with her until she was able to leave and then take her to his own home to convalesce. We all found this rather exciting and obviously contacted Mul Yong and told her about the situation. She was all for coming to visit her mother before she had the operation.

Dad suggested that she might want to wait until her mother had recovered from the operation and could see her daughter properly. He also explained that she was not in good health after years of a near-starvation diet. He was hoping that good food and rest would improve her health. Mul Yong reluctantly agreed and Dad said that he would let her know when Mi Yong was up to seeing her. He would even send me to pick Mul Yong up from the airport when it was time.

So much had happened since that March day. It was now mid-May and so many secrets had been revealed through Granddad Johnny's 'black book'.

Dad was picked up by his driver and taken to Heathrow Airport Terminal 5 to pick Mi Yong up and take her to a private hospital in the centre of London. He was to stay with her until she was ready to leave. Before Dad left home, he said that he was rather puzzled because the intelligence service had allocated bodyguards to give close protection to Mi Yong. They would join Dad in picking her up at the airport and follow in a separate vehicle to the hospital. He thought that there were some political intrigues evolving because of Cheondung Yong's position in the North Korean government. He also wished me luck in my up-and-coming mixed martial arts tournament.

# Chapter 10
# Saturday Night's Alright for Fighting

It was going to be a first for me and I really didn't know what to expect! I must admit that I wondered why I thought it was a good idea. Anyway, traditional 'martial arts' fighting has a formality and set protocols that you can get too used to. Perhaps to the detriment of your development! I wanted to find out what it was like to fight someone using full contact. I suppose I wanted to see what it was like to explore the real violence of fighting. Did I have it in me to really fight? The mixed martial arts competition was taking place in a leisure centre near Pontypool. The guy in charge of the Usk dojang volunteered to be my second at the ringside as he had some experience in the discipline. He's called Dom.

For those relatively unaware of what to expect from this kind of fighting, which probably includes me, it is fought either in a cage or in an octagonal ring. The flooring inside the ring is very springy. There are three rounds of no more than three minutes with a minute between each round to take on water and get patched up. There is a referee in the ring who allocates up to 2 penalty points for any offence and three judges who score each round. A judge allocates 10 points to the fighter he or she deems wins the round and 9 points or less to the other fighter. The winner is the fighter who wins the most rounds or accumulates the most points over the three. There is also a win if the opponent is disqualified, submits or is knocked out. The idea of knocking-out someone sends shivers down my spine, as it isn't something I would really want to do to anyone.

Perhaps that reluctance will be tested! I am fighting in the 'featherweight' category; which is a weight that falls between 144lbs–155lbs. The female combatants wear shorts and a vest. Open-fingered, lightweight gloves are worn for punching. There are no head-guards. Females are allowed to wear chest protectors under their vests and a mouth-guard. This fighting incorporates all types of martial arts. To be successful, a fighter needs to be skilled in: kicking, punching, grappling, throwing, strangle-holds, joint-holds, and groundwork. Boxers, wrestlers and Brazilian jujitsu exponents seem to be the most successful fighters presently. The referee will stop a fight if one of the protagonists is clearly being beaten badly. There are a great many rules, believe it or not; too many to list really.

Here are a few—no head-butting, no attacks to the spine, back of the head, eyes, mouth, hair, throat, groin or small joints. You cannot throw an opponent out of the fighting area. You cannot knee, kick or stomp a grounded opponent. You cannot use a downward pointing elbow strike or drive an opponent into the canvas onto their head or neck. You can punch a person repeatedly if they are on the ground. Something again that I'm a little concerned about.

Before the fight, there was a weigh-in to make absolutely certain that we were fighting in the correct weight category. An assigned medic also examined each fighter. A urine sample had to be submitted before the fight and was tested there and then to establish whether a fighter was taking illegal substances. The doctor checked out my eyes, took my temperature and examined my head for bumps; hands, feet, knees and elbows were examined as to their soundness. After the fight, each fighter would be examined again in case of signs of concussion. Oh, and we also had to submit to a pregnancy test. I have to admit that the thoroughness was impressive. This tournament was strongly advocating the need to safeguard the competitors.

The fight took place in an octagonal ring. The noise from the tiered stands was overwhelming. As I peered out from my stool with Dom kneeling in front of me giving last-minute instructions, I couldn't help but feel that I had made a poor judgement call. I had to shake the negativity; otherwise, there would be only one outcome. Whilst pumping with adrenaline and excitement that I only reserved for fight situations I scanned the scene. Outside the gladiatorial ring, the crowd were baying to be entertained. Outside the ropes, the seconds were preparing themselves for the one-minute round breaks. I could smell the stale sweat and ferrous smell of the blood of earlier combatants emanating from the canvas like an invisible assault on my olfactory senses. Water, sponges, ice-packs, wipes and towels were all being checked by the seconds and then all was ready for action.

I took a long look at my opponent who was sitting on a stool in the opposite corner to me. She seemed to be in a jumpy, agitated state. She constantly moved her legs, bashing one fist onto an open palm. Her face was quite long in relation to the shortness of her torso and lower limbs. She seemed to have a lopsided mouth which curled into a snarl. She had a wild look in her eyes and was staring at me with pure hatred; as if I were her next meal! I wasn't interested in that. I was good at compartmentalising my thoughts. I wanted to have a look at her physique to gain some knowledge of her potential attributes and weaknesses. She appeared to be short and stocky. Very powerful muscular shoulders led down to weight-trained arms with clearly defined triceps and biceps. Her arms, whilst muscular, were not long.

Attacking her with punches using my much greater arm length might be wise in the initial stages. She looked as if she punched in the shoulders. Grappling with her might be worth avoiding. Her legs were very muscular and I sensed that she had explosive energy that could be dangerous. Having analysed her physically, I surmised that she might like to use her fists to soften up her opponent and then move in close, attempt a throw and move into groundwork. On the ground, she would be a formidable fighter. I knew that it was fatal to start a fight with a set plan and that I had to evolve my strategy whilst learning about her through the movements she made in the opening encounters.

The 'Master of Ceremonies' (MC) climbed into the ring, with a microphone in his left hand and drew everyone's attention. We both stood up in anticipation of the fight about to begin. Dom tapped me on the shoulder and muttered 'good luck and stay alert'. When the MC reached the centre of the ring, he raised the microphone and in too loud a voice said, "Our next bout in this evening's martial entertainment is a featherweight contest of three rounds of three minutes. In the blue corner, from Hereford, is Kerry 'Mighty' Morgan on her debut in the sport. (Faint, polite ripple of applause mixed with jeers and laughter!) In the red corner from Pontardawe, near Swansea, with ten knockout wins out of ten is Samantha 'Smiler' Vaughan'. (Frenetic applause, shouts of encouragement and derisory remarks about me her opponent)."

At that point, the MC exited the ring and the referee entered. He called us both forward and closely inspected our gloves. He then stepped away and circled us whilst saying 'fight'. We both respectfully touched gloves and the fight was on. I bounced backwards onto my toes, fists up with my left hand pronouncing that I was a southpaw (someone who leads with their left hand). Smiler Vaughan took two right-footed strides forward and launched a right-handed looping punch at my head. It was a vicious hay-maker but I had reacted instinctively and double shuffled smoothly to my right. It was good to know. She was a dangerous street brawler. I moved in with my long reach and jabbed multiple times first to her head and then to her body. She used her hands and arms effectively to protect her face and body.

It felt good not to have to pull my punches. Tempo or cadence is important in a fight situation. I wanted to give the impression that I was a fight novice so I moved at a much slower speed, occasionally lifting my leg up to block a feint, arms and hands fending off punches, and generally giving ground. I had to be offensive in my movements but kicks were deliberately languorous and always lacking penetration and distance. I wanted her to think I was a complete sucker. I watched carefully. Very often accomplished fighters have trouble with beginners because tempo is hesitant and accidental. An experienced fighter can become hypnotised by the inertia. Her face was set in a determined grimace and I observed a movement pattern which hinted at a future attack. Her right foot kept on double tapping the ground as if she was waiting for an opening.

I decided to give the opening to her and dropped both arms to my sides and bounced into range. Her eyes narrowed and her mouth formed into a snarl. I led with my chin to make sure she would take the bait. She anticipated my stepping back out of punching range and with a double tap of her right foot launched a roundhouse kick directed at the left side of my head. I accelerated my movement, slipped my head inside her attack without moving my body and was able to lance my right elbow into her left upper pectoral muscle and imbalance her to the right. Whilst her kicking leg was aimed at my left shoulder, I moved forward rapidly at a ninety-degree angle into 'ouchigari' and swept her standing leg away. I took her to the ground landing on her heavily and punched her repeatedly in the face and body. The force of her landing from so high with me on top of her really took the wind out of her and she blew her mouth-guard out with an 'oomph'.

She was in shock from the impact and my accelerated movements. She was slow to respond so I capitalised on this by positioning my right arm beneath her right arm just above the elbow joint and levering upwards whilst holding her right wrist with my left hand. She was in an awkward situation. The referee came in. I could feel her body jerking to extricate herself. If I continued, she would break her own arm. I could sense her realisation that she couldn't break out from the hold. She tapped the floor with her feet and at that point, the referee decided to call it. I had won! I slowly allowed the outside world into my consciousness. Surprisingly, the partisan crowd were very quiet as I released 'Smiler Vaughan'.

However, as I moved back to my corner to await the official verdict, slowly but surely the applause grew in intensity. Dom said, "You could have at least given the fans a round of entertainment!"

I smiled ruefully and retorted, "She's too dangerous for that. The longer it went on, the more likely she would have absolutely destroyed me!"

The MC re-entered the ring and made the announcement. I went with Dom to visit the fight doctor who examined me and pronounced a clean bill of health. The fight organiser stopped me on the way and asked if I would be interested in further fights but to make them longer next time. I told him I would have a think and get back to him. I thanked Dom for his assistance and told him I would be at the Usk dojang the following week. I returned to my dressing room. I showered and whilst heading back to my car overheard Dom, who was still chatting to the fight organiser about me, say, "Kerry sees fighting as an 'art' form. She is interested in challenging herself and improving her skills. I suppose you could say she is a 'purist'."

Whilst driving back to Hereford, I evaluated the experience and decided that it wasn't for me. Perhaps I was being too 'high and mighty' about it but for some reason, I found the experience made me feel very uncomfortable. I'm sure some psycho-analysis would clarify what made me feel that way. Hey, my gut feeling would suffice. When I got home, everyone wanted to know about what had happened. I told them briefly, had something to eat and went to bed. I always find that adrenaline has a way of not letting you sleep so I tossed and turned and woke up the next day feeling pretty groggy.

Life goes on, but after that experience, I didn't like the idea of fighting people for the gratification of others. It felt like a form of manipulation that I didn't feel comfortable with. After every fight, I generally go into analysing every move and just make visual improvements for the next time. I decided to contact Mul Yong that evening after school and ask her about her experiences in 'mixed martial arts'.

When I got home, I heard that Dad had phoned Mum and informed her that Mi Yong was ready to leave the hospital and would be convalescing with us. He asked that I communicate this to Mul Yong and also tell her that her mum was absolutely desperate to meet her and that she was welcome to stay with us in Hereford. I, of course, gave this information to Mul Yong, forgetting to ask about her mixed martial arts experiences in all the excitement. Well, I could talk to her about that on the way from the airport.

*This is her response:*

*Dear Kerry,*

*I am so excited. To see my mother at last! I will book a flight from Houston to Heathrow as soon as is physically possible. I'll need to make arrangements for others to oversee my three schools whilst I'm away. I'll also ask a neighbour to water my house-plants. Oh, how exciting! Will you be picking me up? I'll send you my flight number, landing time and terminal number when I've booked. How long should I reasonably stay for? Can I pay you in advance for my board and lodge with your kind family? Apologies for gabbling but*

*I'm so overwhelmed with it all. Anyway, I need to get on the internet and book the flight so I'll stop! Oh also, where is Hereford? I thought you came from Llanelli in Wales. Another question I've been pondering is, will my presence upset my father's wife?*

*Regards*
*Mul Yong*

Wow! She was so excited! The last question caused me some concern. I went to speak to Mum about the three questions we could answer. Mum thought that 'how long she could stay' was really open-ended. About the 'board and lodge', Mum didn't feel a contribution was necessary as Mul Yong could earn her keep by helping out with the washing up and cooking. About Nan's response to Mi Yong and Mul Yong's presence, she thought that Mildred would always be polite and respectful and anyway they didn't have to meet Nan if they didn't feel it was appropriate. I relayed this to Mul Yong and she was very pleased with our response.

I explained where Hereford was and the fact that Granddad Johnny and Dad's brothers had remained near the areas where they had been born.

# Chapter 11
# Visitors

Dad arrived the following morning with Mi Yong. It was Saturday. Granddad was 26 years old in 1951 and Mi Yong around 18 years of age—that would make her 85 or thereabouts. Seven years older than Nanny Mildred. Well, she didn't look her age. She was about 5ft 3 inches in height, slim, held herself erect and moved her slight frame with fluidity and awareness. We all greeted her enthusiastically with hugs which seemed to take her aback. We went into the bungalow and sat in the kitchen. Tea and biscuits were served. She had very brown eyes, almost black; she had very short, jet-black hair, streaked with silver. Whilst her face was wrinkled with age, she had a mischievous sparkle in her eyes with laughter seemingly ready to burst out of her at any moment.

Dad made the introductions. She drank Jasmine tea and nibbled on a rich tea biscuit. It seemed to me that we were in awe of her. She had fought for her beloved country and had paid the price of being taken into exile for most of her life. She had been the prisoner of a communist state that crushed dissidents and had survived, yet she still appeared to have the capacity to smile and laugh at life's joys. She spoke haltingly in an American accent. Dad explained that whilst she spoke

English she was very rusty because of the infrequency of use. Her son spoke English well but his work kept him away from his mother a great deal. She would understand if we spoke a little more slowly as our accents were somewhat unfamiliar to her. She did thank us though for taking her into our home. She was still getting used to seeing clearly out of both eyes and constantly looked around to see the new world she had been placed in.

I certainly wanted to ask her lots of questions about her life and I'm sure Liam and Rhianna felt the same. It was as if we had a famous person in our house all to ourselves. However, Dad made it clear, very subtly, that Mi Yong was tired after her long journey and would need to rest up. Mi Yong was given a tour of the bungalow by Dad and shown the room she would be staying in. She decided to rest her eyes so remained in the room with the curtains closed. At lunchtime, she joined us in the kitchen and offered to help my mum prepare food. My mum insisted she should sit down. Mi Yong was much chattier and asked us individually about ourselves which also gave me the opportunity to talk about the contents of Granddad's black book and the information he had divulged about Mi Yong and Mul Yong with Dad subsequently tracking down the whereabouts of both of them.

After lunch, Mi Yong asked if she could exercise outside as it was such a fine day so my dad showed her our patio area around the back of the house. She went to her room and then returned to the patio dressed in loose-fitting plain clothing and she was bare-footed. Dad, Liam and I watched from the side. She started with light stretching and breathing exercises. She then moved into her forms. She closed her eyes and started, what I could only describe as a dance; the movements were extremely smooth without juddering or hesitation. All her movement seemed to come from her legs and she moved in circles, sometimes with wide legs, other times with hip-width leg movements. It was beautiful! Her arms also seemed to follow a circular route in conjunction with her leg movements. It was effortless! She attacked and defended against an imaginary opponent. She rarely punched but slapped, chopped or used the heel of her hand.

When she turned away, she would use her elbow to strike. Her leg movements included kicks from the upper foot, heels and knees, left or right, it didn't seem to matter. Her balance was perfect! The kicks were aimed mainly at knee level, just below the patella, and seemed to be a taught strategy to dissuade an opponent from attacking with the feet. She simulated tripping movements whilst using her arms to propel the imaginary body part to the sides, backwards, forwards and over her own body in a movement of positional sacrifice. Whilst fluid, the speed of movement could be exceedingly fast and then very slow! She practised for forty minutes! When she stopped, she wasn't even out of breath! I have to admit the routine she performed was awesome. I nearly gave her a round of applause.

After she had warmed down, I asked her about the routine and what martial arts style it was. She considered the question for a moment and replied almost in a whisper, "It is a hybrid of Taekkyon and Subak. I paused at your question because I aspire to have no style when fighting, although my forms reflect the styles I have been taught since I was a child. The royal court instructor, Myung-Duk, who your Grandad Johnny knew at Kwanumsa Temple, remained my instructor and guardian all his life and my training is still dedicated to his memory." I asked what happened to him.

Her reply was heartfelt, "He was killed by the enemy at the temple. By all accounts, he took many lives, in an effort to protect my babies! Myung-Duk's wife managed to hide away from the enemy with Mul Yong in a baby basket whilst my brother was captured carrying away Cheondung. I was in another part of the camp when the attack came and whilst trying to return to my children, I was captured by the Chinese. I was later reunited with my brother and my baby boy in an internment camp. I suppose we were lucky not to be shot. It is only because we are members of the Korean royal family that they resisted the temptation. I never saw Myung-Duk, his wife or my daughter again.

I asked about others who had escaped but there were very few and no one seemed to know what had happened to Mul Yong. The enemy used us in their propaganda with western powers to demonstrate how merciful communists could be to their enemy. They tried very hard indeed to re-educate me. I was tortured physically and mentally but my spirit did not break. I am scarred externally but I like to think I have retained who I really am inside. I am very sorry to hear that Johnny has passed away. He was a good man and I remember our short time together fondly. Now tomorrow would you like to fight with me? I'll go easy on you, I promise!"

Well, I was taken aback by that and could only nod in agreement. Whilst smiling and winking, Dad said jokingly, "It's not often that Kerry is lost for words."

Mi Yong had the evening meal with us and she was the life and soul of the party. She explained that she didn't often have a chance to converse with people and that she led a solitary existence. Soon after, exhausted, I believe from probably talking so much, she retired to her room. I went online to check out Taekkyeon and Subak as I was unfamiliar with them as martial arts systems. It seems that Taekkyeon is a cultural 'treasure' of Korea.

That evening, I received a WhatsApp message from Mul Yong stating that her flight from Houston would land at Heathrow Airport Terminal Five, on the following Saturday morning at 9:50 am. That was in a week's time. Her message oozed excitement and a little uncertainty. I replied and said that I had watched her mum performing her martial arts routines and felt that they would get on with each other really well. I also stated that her mum had offered to spar with me the next day. In an amused response, she asked me not to hurt Mi Yong before she saw her. I told Mul Yong, encouragingly, that it was unlikely I would even make the lightest of contacts as she moved so quickly. She seemed to be pleased by my comments!

I sparred with Mi Yong in the garage the following Sunday morning before breakfast. It's a large double garage with 'dojang' mats on the floor. As a family, we sparred with each other often, although Mum and Dad said that they were getting too old! Well, everybody was keen to watch us spar. Mi Yong wore loose clothing like before but this time had each foot bound in a white fabric tied at each ankle. I wore the same kit as I had worn at the mixed martial arts tournament: shorts and vest; gum shield. Before we began, I asked if it was semi-contact or full contact. Mi Yong smiled enigmatically and with a twinkle in her eye said, "Let us see how things evolve, shall we!"

In my mind, I was saying to myself that I had to go easy on her because if I did strike her, I could end up killing her. After all, she was an octogenarian! Is that ageist? So, I would definitely hold back on my strikes and just gently make contact. Hah, how foolish I was! We bowed and touched fists and before I knew it, she had slapped me gently across my left cheek. I looked at her with indignant surprise. She just chuckled mischievously. Now our fighting styles were in complete contrast. My style, if it was to be analysed was that of a fencer, up on my toes using my hands and feet as sword substitutes; always leading with left side or right with lunging or short steps, fists placed like a boxer. Mi Yong moved her feet in a more rotational way, hence like a dance, whilst her arms constantly moved in a rotation. Sometimes short movements sometimes extended.

Interestingly, she never took her eyes away from mine. I tried a reverse roundhouse aimed at the left side of her head. She brushed the strike firmly away with an open left hand, stepped quickly in and slapped me, gently, with her left hand on the same cheek again. I tried a combination of punches, left jab, right jab, aimed at her face and then an uppercut. She weaved and bobbed avoiding my direct attacks easily. Whenever I attacked with my left or right leg, she had a way of targeting my standing leg with trips, sweeps or a heel to just under the kneecap. Yes, it did really hurt! I tried combinations of kicks and punches but she always managed to either step away or come very close very quickly and gently slap me on the face. I tried not to be agitated by this but it did have a strong effect on my confidence. Punches were either avoided or swept to the left or right powerfully. "You are trying too hard," she stated at one point. "It is affecting your balance and fluidity. Try to calm yourself!"

Her words washed over me, but I wasn't able to process them so intent was I on making at least some contact with her. She came inside my arm defence and struck me with the heels of both hands on either side of my sternum. The shove knocked me back eighteen inches and in that moment, she filled the space and grabbed hold of my bra straps. She dropped her left leg between my legs, hopped into the air, bent her right throwing leg, making contact with my midriff and sat her buttocks between my legs whilst pulling my upper body over with her arms, she then straightened her right leg sharply and launched me over her head with ease. The sacrificial throw 'tomoenage' was perfectly demonstrated. I landed a little heavily and was still in shock from the speed of successive attacks.

Mi Yong came over and helped me up. She then went back to the centre of the mat and waited for me to compose myself before bowing. I did the same. She came to me and congratulated me on my aggressiveness. Dad came over and winked at me and said, "Not bad considering Mi Yong has in sixty years tutored some of the world's greatest martial arts exponents."

We had glasses of squash and rich tea biscuits and whilst I was munching away Mi Yong added, "Look to a person's eyes to see what they intend to do with their bodies. It takes many years to perceive the nuances but in the split second, before they move, you can determine their course of action. That was great fun! Can we do it again tomorrow and I'll teach you about perception in combat." Mi Yong started to chuckle to herself and I asked her what was funny. "For the last fifteen years or so, the sight in my left eye has been deteriorating rapidly. It's quite hard to fight with only one good eye and here I am talking about perception! Anyway, it's so good to have full vision again."

So, from then on, before I went to college each morning, I sparred with Mi Yong. She showed me, quite meticulously, how to blend different combat forms so my fighting style was more fluid. We broke movements down and spoke about the different techniques that could be employed to throw, trip, sweep, punch, kick, choke and lock, so as to maintain fluidity and balance. All practitioners needed to get away from the rigidity and conformity of traditional martial arts systems. I felt that my style benefitted from the insight and I was moving towards a more multi-dimensional form of combat. She was very philosophical and spoke often about how we should seek inner peace when fighting and that in reality, we were not fighting an opponent but our inner self. Our ultimate goal as martial artists should be to attain 'no form, no style and no art'.

I asked Mi Yong about what Dad had said about her tutoring the top martial artists but all she would say was that they came to her in confidence and she was a discrete person who would not betray a trust. I asked how Dad knew then! "My son, Cheondung, likes to boast to others about how capable I am for my age. Sweet really, but I have told him not to," she responded. I asked if he was an accomplished martial artist and her reply came with a chuckle, "He doesn't practise enough! He's an important man, always working, with little time for leisure activities, his words! He was very good as a child and young man but when he became involved in politics, all his free time just disappeared. He does, however, live to unify the country of Korea. He is totally committed to that one aim. In my opinion, a desire that could get him killed. Nevertheless, he keeps on trying to build bridges only for Kim and others to knock them down.

Cheondung has worked hard, with others, to reduce the present tensions between North Korea and the South and, of course, the United States over nuclear testing and the threat of inter-continental missiles. His group has encouraged Kim to resume relations with the south and even suggested that the Olympics in Seoul in February were an opportunity to develop relationships with the south and subsequently, the United States. The two countries did agree to field a combined women's ice hockey team which is a move forward and a delegation from North Korea, fronted by Kim's sister, did attend the games. However, Kim has to appear strong, and there are many factions in the government that see Cheongdung's group as weak and too pro-west. He needs to watch his back. He took an immense risk getting me out of the north and unfortunately, he is beholding to the South Korean, American and British governments.

If Kim finds out, which is likely, then Cheondung will end up at best in an internment camp for political prisoners. At worse, public execution! Oh, I do hope that boy knows what he is doing! Anyway, I swore to myself that I wouldn't talk politics whilst staying with such a lovely family. I must be quiet."

After a moment's thought, I asked in a puzzled tone, "How come these famous martial artists were able to come to visit you in North Korea? Surely, they would not be allowed!"

Mi Yong thought it a very interesting question before responding with, "Kim, likes the attention from the west. He likes to mix with the rich and famous and these people will pay quite large sums of money to say they have visited the enigmatic country of North Korea and spent time with its exalted great leader. That coupled with the opportunity to be taught by an exponent of quite a rare 'martial art' form is an enticement too much for people with plenty of money! Like many dictators, he has one rule for the people and another for himself. He speaks perfectly good English, just like me, with an American accent! He pretends to be many things, but he is an astute person who should never be underestimated."

Mi Yong, at our family evening meal, asked about Mul Yong. We filled her in on what information Mul Yong had told us about her life. Mi Yong was puzzled by why she had been abandoned in a wicker basket by the carved door of the temple. Also, why was there a note giving information about the child's parentage and name? It suggested that the adult leaving the child was prepared for the desertion. Mi Yong did not think that Myung-Duk's wife would do such a thing; unless she had been forced to make that decision because her own situation was endangered. Mi Yong, also wondered aloud, why the phrase, 'probably American' had been ascribed to the child's father. Everyone at Kwanumsa Temple knew that Johnny was British. She went on to say, "It's not as if there is anyone alive that could clarify the events surrounding that puzzle."

At that moment, it occurred to me that I should ask the question of who Mi Yong's father was. She smiled and said that she was one of three children. Her two brothers were much older than her and her father was called Yi Jeon. *Rhianna will be pleased,* I thought to myself!

Monday to Friday went by in a routine of pre-college sparring with Mi Yong, college lessons, evening meals and homework. On Wednesday, I visited the Usk dojang with Dad. He was still convalescing so didn't take part. I sparred with some of the senior fighters and was asked if something had changed in my life as my fighting had evolved considerably. I was very pleased by the comments. I had obviously been assimilating Mi Yong's teaching.

On Friday evening, I asked Dad if I should invite Mi Yong to come with me to Heathrow to collect Mul Yong. He was unsure. "Perhaps, you should ask Mi Yong's opinion," he suggested.

I asked her and after some moments of thought, she replied, "I don't think meeting Mul Yong for the first time, since she was a newborn baby, at an airport, is the best introduction for either of us. However, what do you think?" I said that they needed to sit with each other for some time as I was sure Mul Yong had many questions for Mi Yong. It was inappropriate at the airport when everyone only really wanted to get where they needed to be. She seemed accepting of that.

The next morning, I set out for Heathrow Terminal 5 at seven o'clock. I would stop at Membury Services for a comfort break. From Hereford, the journey took approximately 2 hours 30 minutes. I had 'WhatsApped' Mul Yong stating that I would stand in the area just outside where she had to walk through and I would hold up a sign saying, 'Water Dragon'. She thought that was very amusing as no one knew her by that name in the United States! She went on to say that because she was a 'stubborn' fighter and would never give in, she had been given the nickname 'Mule' which I thought was very funny. I also asked if she wanted me to have a coffee waiting for her when she came through. She thought that was very kind of me and yes she would! I did do a comfort stop at Membury, but I have to admit I was too excited to stay longer for a coffee.

I arrived at Terminal 5 short-term parking at nine-thirty, parked up and went to have a coffee. The coffee outlet was very close to where passengers came out of the baggage collection area so I sat there and people-watched whilst keeping an eye on the flight arrivals monitor. Her flight landed on time. I thought half an hour to get through customs and collect her luggage would be pretty average so I bought a coffee at 10:20 and strolled over to the arrivals exit point. It was all quiet there. I put Mul Yong's coffee by my feet, pulled the sign out from the inside breast pocket of my coat and hung it around my neck. A small trickle of passengers started drifting past. Some looked bewildered whilst others walked confidently and with assurance through.

Clearly, multiple planes had landed for very soon that trickle turned into a flood. I had to be vigilant now! There were so many bodies with baggage going passed and the people waiting seemed to jostle for the best positions. Also, like me, there were people holding up name boards and looking keenly for the unknown face. Suddenly, someone tapped me on the shoulder, I turned, and 'the someone' said, "You must be Kerry!"

I instinctively put my arms around Mul Yong, who was as tall as me, and said, "Welcome to the UK! I've got you a latte," and handed it over. She thanked me and asked if we could sort out how much she owed me later. We headed for the short stay carpark. I paid at the ticket machine. As usual, the prices were outrageous and we headed off. Mul Yong was very engaging and chatted to me as if we had known each other all our lives. She spoke about the annoying and nice passengers on the flight. The food! Her inability to sleep because she was so excited. She acted like more of a teenager than me. She kept on smiling. It wasn't a false smile either. She was genuinely pleased to meet me. I couldn't help but be affected by her charm and also smiled inanely. Driving and chatting for a relatively inexperienced driver is quite hard so I ended up listening and giving the occasional response.

We stopped at Newbury Services for some hot food and a drink. It was really the first time I could really take a look at her. She certainly did not look like a 66-year-old. Her skin was vibrantly healthy looking as was her very dark brown hair. She was lean and did not carry any excess weight that I could see. Yes, she obviously looked Korean but her eyes were green, sparkling and lively. She had that cute dimple on her chin that was so reminiscent of Granddad Johnny's. Having seen her mum, Mi Yong, I could say that she had both parents' characteristics. Her accent, a Texan twang, seemed completely at odds with her Asian appearance. She certainly drew looks when we entered the service station's eating area. After buying some hot food, we sat opposite each other in some comfortable chairs. She chose a cheeseburger and fries and a Diet Coke whilst I had cod and chips with a tango. She told me that she normally was very strict about her diet and rarely had 'carbs'.

As she was on holiday, she felt that she could go off her strict regime. I asked her about America and the city of Houston. I told her that she was the second American that I had met; Tom Bonilla being the first. This is what she said, "Houston has a population of two million. I live in a suburb called 'Spring Branch' which has a high-density population of multi-ethnicity, particularly Hispanics and Asians. A lot of Korean people settled there in the 50s and 60s. These days, the area is a family-friendly suburb with wide-ranging food outlets, good schools and plenty of parks for walking and recreation. I have a two-bedroom flat there and it is a relatively quiet street that I live in. Most of my neighbours are elderly. Come to think of it, I must be one of them! Ha, you don't realise that you are getting older! My martial arts schools are in the same area, really for convenience's sake, as believe me, the traffic is absolutely appalling and getting anywhere takes forever."

"Oh, it's really bad in Hereford as well! I interjected."

"Um…where is Hereford in relation to Heathrow," Mul Yong asked.

"Well, it's two hours thirty minutes by car. If you were to look at a map, we travel west along a motorway called the M4 until we exit at a place called Swindon in the county of Wiltshire. We travel then in a north-westerly direction passing Cirencester and Gloucester. The area is called the 'Cotswolds' and it is renowned for its lovely villages, where the houses are made of creamy stone. Our ultimate destination is the county of Herefordshire which is famous for black and white Jacobean houses. It is a very rural county with farming of all sorts and cider-making being the main sources of income. You must have heard of 'Hereford' cattle being from Texas?"

"Yes, I have done some research," came Mul Yong's amused reply.

I continued, "The county has a population of approximately 192,000 people in an area of 212 square miles, with Hereford city having 56,000 as residents."

"Wow, that's not a lot of people for such a large area. I think approximately 135,000 live in Spring Branch, and that's 40 square miles," she said in surprise.

We finished our food, used the toilets and headed on our way. After leaving the motorway and the busy roads around Swindon, we saw the open countryside of the Cotswolds. Mul Yong thought the landscape was so green and the stone walls separating the fields were so attractive. As we approached 'The Air-balloon' Pub at the top of Birdlip, I glanced at Mul Yong, as she had stopped talking, only to see that she had fallen asleep and was gently snoring with her mouth open. I sighed and smiled whilst saying to myself quietly, "It's quite hard being a tour guide!"

The Gloucester bypass was its usual busy self but traffic was reduced greatly after I got on the road to Newent. We stopped at the Trumpet Inn for a comfort break and a hot drink. Mul Yong apologised for falling asleep and not keeping me company. I told her not to worry and that we would arrive in 15 minutes. She said that she was very nervous about meeting her mother and did not know what to say to her. I suggested that she be herself and just give her a hug and take it from there! I told her that my dealings with her mum had led me to believe that she was a compassionate and kind woman who had remained so even after life had dealt her many terrible experiences. I also added that if Mul Yong felt uncertain as to what to say and do then how would Mi Yong, a mother who hadn't seen her child for 66 years, and had probably given up any hope of ever seeing her, feel?

That did make her pause and reflect. Anyway, she was beginning to make me feel nervous for them both. We pulled up onto the drive and Mum, Dad, Liam and Rhianna were there to greet us, but no Mi Yong. They each gave Mul Yong a hug and welcomed her. Rhianna took her suitcase into the bungalow whilst we followed. We went into the kitchen and had hot drinks and biscuits. After the introductions and some small talk about the flight and journey from Heathrow, Dad said, "I expect you're wondering why Mi Yong didn't meet you on arrival!" Mul Yong nodded. "Well, she is finding the anticipation of your arrival so overwhelming that she has gone to meditate and practise her 'forms' in the garage. She thought that you might like to join her when you've freshened up."

I smiled at Muy Yong and whispered, "There, you're not the only one who's nervous. Perhaps, the both of you doing something you understand will make meeting each other for the first time easier for you!" And they say wisdom is wasted on the youth, pah! I took Mul Yong to the en suite bedroom she would share with Mi Yong. She unpacked her clothes, had a quick wash and changed into loose clothing to practise her 'forms'. I then took her to the garage and cheerily said, "Good luck, I'm sure it'll be fine!"

I went back into the bungalow and chatted with the others. They all seemed a little on edge and concerned. Dad said, "I hope to goodness the two of them get along as if they decide not to like each other they could wreck the garage!"

I laughed and said, "They'll be fine. Neither of them realises it yet, but they are very alike. At present, they are both emotionally charged. I think Mul Yong is angry; not necessarily with her mother but with the situation that life threw at them. The bottom line is she is very happy that she now knows who her dad was; she has a mother who is still alive and a twin brother. Remember, if you hadn't contacted her, her parentage would have remained a mystery for the rest of her life. Also, a big bonus, us, a family that she didn't even know she had. She's a really nice person with a wicked sense of humour.

As for Mi Yong, she seems to accept what life has thrown at her and through it all has remained positive. I know she feels guilty for not having found Mul Yong, even though she was not in a position to do so. I think it's a pretty good idea for them to meet doing something that they both find so much solace in."

About an hour and a half later, they both emerged from the garage hand-in-hand smiling happily. Mi Yong was the first to speak, "As you can imagine, we had a lot to talk about. We've talked out anger and guilt and it has helped both of us understand the other a little better."

Mul Yong continued by saying, "We would both like to thank you, our newfound family, for bringing us together. Alan risked his life to bring my mother out of North Korea which we will always be grateful for. If Kerry hadn't bothered to read my father's 'black book', tragically none of us would ever have met. Thank you all so much for your welcoming hearts." I think we were all relieved that their first meeting had ended amicably. We all had lunch together and the 'banter' around the table was jolly and full of fun.

Mul Yong had a sleep in the afternoon whilst I did some revision! My 'A' levels would begin tomorrow. At our evening meal, Dad asked them if they had any thoughts about some touristy things they would like to do. Mi Yong became quite excited and stated that she had always wanted to experience a quintessentially English afternoon tea. Mul Yong also thought it a good idea. They both also thought that as they were in the United Kingdom they should experience some historical settings like stately homes and castles. They were keen to meet the rest of the family and visit Granddad Johnny's grave. Mul Yong also was interested in visiting the 'dojangs' in Usk and Llanelli.

Mum and Dad both agreed that they would escort our two visitors on daily trips out and an itinerary would be drawn up. My focus had to be, for the next three weeks at least, concentrating on my exams. My English constituted two papers of 2 hours 30 minutes; Religious Studies a whopping four papers of 2 hours each; PE just one paper of two hours. I asked Mi Yong if I could have some more tuition from her and it was agreed that we would train together before breakfast each morning. She felt that it would make me even more alert for sitting the exams. Each evening at dinner either Mi Yong or Mul Yong would relate the day's events.

On Monday, the four of them went to Abergavenny for afternoon tea at 'The Angel Hotel'. Apparently, the tea, sandwiches and cakes were 'scrummy'—Mul Yong's words. On Tuesday morning, Mum and Dad took them on the 'black and white houses' village trail stopping for lunch at 'Jules' in Weobley. In the afternoon, they visited the Black and White House and then Hereford Cathedral. The both of them apparently stood in awe of the building. Dad even organised someone to take them around and tell them about the history of the building whilst he and Mum went for a coffee outside in the courtyard. When they had concluded the conducted tour, Dad took them to the SAS stained glass window opposite the main entrance to the cathedral and explained that his dad Johnny had been a member of the regiment from 1947 to 1965. The window was inaugurated in 2016 to commemorate 75 years since the SAS had been formed. The stained glass windows are titled 'Ascension' and the glass consists of 3000 pieces of 40 different colours.

Mi Yong thought the windows held a poignancy that reflected the transience of human life which she found sad, but at the same time uplifting. She was particularly struck by the quotation: *We are the Pilgrims, master; we shall go Always a little further; it may be Beyond that last blue mountain barred with snow; Across that angry or that glimmering sea.* (James Elroy Flecker 1884–1915). Mi Yong felt that the term 'pilgrim' applied to her and the sentiment of continuing to endure against all odds, which she gleaned from the words, struck a very deep chord in her psyche. Dad further explained that at the SAS camp, there was a 'clock tower' with the names of all regimental soldiers who had died in various conflicts and that the quotation was also there.

I asked him, "How do you know that?"

"Well, I have visited there occasionally, perhaps more than occasionally but as you know I can't talk about it," was his apologetic response. He also added that James Elroy Flecker, whilst gaining eminence as a poet, had attended both Oxford and Cambridge as a student and had died at the age of 31. Academics felt that Flecker would have attained the same status as John Keats if he had lived a longer life. You learn something new every day! Our two guests raved about their day during the evening meal. Mi Yong was so enthused by the cathedral that she wanted to walk down on her own the following morning. I was quizzed about my first Religious Studies paper by Mum and Dad. I said that the questions needed serious analysis as it was easy to be diverted from the true focus, but I thought I had done reasonably well.

Before breakfast on Wednesday morning, I trained with Mi Yong and 'Mule'. Mul Yong insisted the night before that we all start calling her by that name as that was what all her friends called her. They had both obviously discussed my fighting style as they both thought that for the rest of the week, they would concentrate on finger, hand, elbow and forearm striking techniques. So the next morning and for the rest of the week, for 40 minutes, I practised striking with my upper limbs in very close combat. We started out in slow motion but then with increased speed and power. We worked through an array of counter moves to different attacks. Mule and Mi Yong promoted the idea that the power of an opponent should be diverted back at them; always with the intention of preserving your own energy.

My revision and attendance at exams continued whilst Mum and Dad took the two ladies out exploring the countryside of Herefordshire and beyond. They went to Stratford upon Avon, Warwick Castle, Hay-on-Wye and Cardiff over the next week. They were astonished at the rich history the UK has. It was beginning to be increasingly noticeable how close mother and daughter were becoming. Dad was also getting fitter and began to do some driving on their outings. Mule and Mi Yong kept on asking about attending Granddad Johnny's grave and meeting Nan. Discussion had also ensued as to when Mule would return to the United States and about Mi Yong's future intentions.

# Chapter 12
# A Nightmare of the Past

We had a visit from Philip Morgan the following week. He had been spending time with Nan. 'Getting to know each other' as he put it. He had also brought back the 'black book' from Nan having read the entire contents. He was interested in reading what I had written about Granddad's story. I considered his request and thought that it would be a good idea to gain another perspective on what I had written. So, I emailed him a copy. He told me that whilst ploughing through the book he had come across an account by Granddad Johnny of the fateful day when Granddad's dad, William, or Bill as he liked to be called, had killed his mum, Annie. Here is what he read:

*When your life is coming to an end, you tend to reflect on it! I'd like to think I've tried to be a good person. 93 years has gone by and I've done a lot of different things in that time. Mildred has been my bedrock. Always so supportive of anything I've wanted to attempt. I love her dearly and go to my demise hoping that she will find someone else to share her remaining days with. No one should be alone. We have brought up three fine young men who are good, honest, independent people.*

*As parents, you always hope that you can bring up your children well, but you don't really know if you've been successful until they have children of their own. Well, I know for certain that we did an excellent job! I also remain hopeful that I see Mul Yong before I pass but I really think it is a forlorn hope. Whilst thinking about this, I've been pondering my own upbringing. There were five of us kids. Mam and Dad were not well off but we did not starve. Peggy, Glenys, Ed and I were very close as children. We looked after each other in school and in the wider world. To be honest, because Philip was fifteen years younger than me, I didn't get to know him as well as I should have. Life often gets so busy that we forget what should be important and with Philip, I should have tried harder to maintain a connection. Anyway, regret is cheap when it is too late to do anything about it!*

*I've been avoiding recollecting what happened on the day my father killed my mother for so long that it has probably damaged me psychologically. I always said to myself that I would never forget the details of that terrible morning but 76 years have passed and my memory isn't as clear as I'd like it to be. I'm afraid that what I'm about to say is rather stark and brutal. It is not intended to give the reader nightmares so I've tried to keep it matter-of-fact with little further detail.*

*I got up at six o'clock that morning as I was due to start a shift at Bynea Steel Works at seven. The Steel Works was only a ten-minute walk away, across Loughor Bridge, from where we lived so I had plenty of time. I started the fire in the sitting room and then shouted Mam, Dad and toddler Philip for breakfast. Within five minutes, Mam was getting breakfast* on. It was scrambled egg on toast. She cut the bread with a large carving knife and left it beside the remains of the loaf. The three of us sat at the table with Philip in his high chair banging a spoon against the wooden table top. It sounded a bit like an irregular drumbeat!

I had noticed that Dad was very quiet and had a strange otherworldly look in his eyes. I asked him if he had slept well but he didn't reply. I asked Mam the same question and she said that Dad had not slept well and had been disturbed by some very vivid nightmares. So much so that he had been covered in a cold sweat, was shivering and had a wild look in his deathly pale face. Mam said he kept repeatedly saying in a pleading sort of way, "You can't make me go back into the woods." She was worried about him and they needed to go to the doctor's that morning. She plated up the scrambled egg on toast and set a plate in front of Dad and then me before starting to sort out Philip's breakfast.

I was sat opposite Dad and as I picked up the salt cellar, something seemed to snap in Dad's mind and he roared fix bayonets and rose so quickly and powerfully that he knocked the four-place table flying, with me going backwards over my over-balancing chair. Fortunately, Philip's high chair was untouched by the explosive eruption of Dad's energy! Dad proceeded to pick up the carving knife off the table and held it in his left hand with his right hand moving to just above his right thigh. Mam helped me up from the floor before heading towards Dad, saying soothingly, "Bill, please put the knife down as you're scaring the children!" His face was set in a snarl and he was clearly living a nightmare without any incursion from the outside reality breaking in. He lunged with *the knife at my mam. She didn't have a chance to avoid the strike and the blade pierced her just under the breast bone.*

*I shouted, "Dad, stop!" I put my hands out in front of me in a defensive but placatory manner. His eyes were glazed and he thrust at me with the knife in the same action he had performed with my mam. The knife went straight through my left hand, burying it up to the hilt, grating the bones in my hand whilst the force continued so that he drove the hand and the blade into my chest to the left side of my sternum. I screamed and keeled over, at which point, he pulled out the knife with his foot on my chest, as if it was attached to a rifle, and plunged it in again. I must have lost consciousness, although my last memory was of Philip screaming at the top of his lungs!*

*I awoke in a hospital bed. I was connected to a lot of machinery and I had tubes sticking out of me. For a boy of seventeen, it was a terrifying awakening. My chest was bandaged with some blood stains showing pinkly. My hand was heavily bandaged as well. I tried to move to a more upright, comfortable position but the pain from my torso was too great. A nurse came in and smiled to see me awake. She asked me if I wanted something to drink and was I comfortable. I asked if I could sit up and she went to ask the matron who then came back with her. They adjusted my position so that I could sit up and brought me a glass of water which they helped me to drink. I asked about my mam and dad but all they could answer was that they were there to attend to my injuries and nothing more. They said that there was a young police officer waiting to take my statement and perhaps he could fill me in on what happened. So they called him and I told him what I remembered about the terrible incident.*

*He wrote everything down and asked me to sign the writing after I had read it back to myself. This I did and then I asked him what had happened to my mam and dad. He said that he didn't think it was his place to say and that a more superior officer should tell me. After he left, I was visited by my two sisters Peggy and Glenys and my brother Ed. The three of them looked visibly shaken and tearful. I whispered, "Please tell me that Mam is alright."*

*The two girls burst into tears and said quietly, "No, she isn't, he killed her!"*

*Ed held my good arm and put his arm around my good shoulder and whispered, "Johnny, you tried your best, but Dad wasn't in that kitchen. He was in the woods at Mametz! He was crazed and berserk from the fear it instilled in him. He was hallucinating and having a nightmare whilst seemingly awake. You and Mam were enemy soldiers that he had to silence so that he and his friends could survive. It's the shrapnel wound getting worse, creating mood swings and hallucinations. He wasn't in his right mind and the police have already told us that the case won't go to court as Dad clearly wasn't of sound mind. The psychologists and doctors have all agreed that he should spend the rest of his life in a mental institution to safeguard the public from him and to also help him. It's terrible that our mam had to die for the medics to do something about his war wound."*

*I asked about Philip and they told me that he was staying with Peggy and her husband. He was still very frightened and had difficulty sleeping at night. I asked what happened after I lost consciousness in the kitchen. Glenys took over and explained that Dad had run out of the house and down Dock Street heading towards the Roman castle remains. "He was covered in blood and many neighbours and other people saw him whilst heading to work. The police were called and he was captured, handcuffed and taken away in a black Mariah van. The next-door neighbour, a lady, saw him coming out of our house in a bewildered-looking way, with blood dripping from a carving knife. She went into our house and saw the carnage Dad had caused. She picked Philip up out of his high chair and went to fetch her husband to see if he could do anything for you or Mam. It was too late for Mam and because of the seriousness of your injuries, he couldn't do much for you. You were not expected to survive. An ambulance was called and you were taken to Glasfryn Hospital in Llanelly."* They all smiled at that and said, *"But, you're a 'Morgan' and we don't give up life that easily!"*

*I had been in hospital for three weeks until that point. My left lung had been perforated twice and there had been bleeding in the chest cavity. I had a number of broken and bruised ribs. They had operated on me to repair the lung. I had to convalesce for another six weeks. After that, I went to visit my dad. He looked a shadow of the man he had been. He was at the time cogent and emotionally distraught. He couldn't look at me at first. His face remained downcast as I made it clear to him that what he had done to Mam and me was beyond his control and that the shrapnel was affecting the reasoning part of his brain creating hallucinations that were perceived by him to be real. He cried and sobbed and said, "I loved her so much! I would never hurt your mam or you! I can only ask for forgiveness but I know that it can't be given. He went on to ask if Philip was alright." I explained that Peggy was looking after Philip. I couldn't take much more of the emotional trauma of the visit so said that I would visit again and left. It was so, so, sad!*

*The following day, I went to the army recruitment office and had a series of tests to determine which branch of the army I should join. A month later, I was doing my basic training with the Royal Electrical and Mechanical Engineers (REME). Whenever I was on leave, I went to visit him. His condition declined rapidly and on my last visit, he was straight-jacketed so he couldn't hurt himself or anyone else. He did not recognise me as the shrapnel had continued to affect his cognition! When I was away in Korea, he died. Ed, Peggy and Glenys organised the funeral and he was buried in Lower Loughor Church next to my mam. I believe that the Mametz Wood action took place in July 1916 so Dad had been carrying that terror around with him for 26 years. I was contacted by a doctor from the hospital Dad had been in and he gave me some of his writing and artwork that the staff had got him to do as a vehicle to dissipate the horrors he had witnessed. I haven't looked too closely at them and at some point, placed them in a drawer in the display cabinet in my lock-up.*

*I know that what I say now, considering what I've written about my life, in this diary, will be hard to believe; but I have been frightened, deep down, for most of my life. That day back in 1942 changed me dramatically. It damaged the confidence I had in myself. I felt ashamed at my inability to save Mam and not forgive Dad. I foolishly blamed myself for Mam's death and not being able to stop Dad. All my actions from then on were associated with a fear of failure and the consequences that could possibly arise from that failure. Not being there when Mi Yong was executed and not being there for Mul Yong has plagued my conscience all my life. If I had been more open and not so secretive, I'm sure outcomes would have been more positive.*

The account came to an abrupt end. What an awful story to keep to yourself for 76 years. There's little doubt that Granddad Johnny must have been a tormented soul, what with the tragedy associated with his parents and the events in Korea. It struck me that Bill Morgan's writing would give further insight into understanding the role that Mametz Wood played on that fateful morning and the choices that were made as a direct result of the tragedy. In fact, the events of that morning had far-reaching consequences that even my generation was now experiencing! I went to tell Dad about what Granddad Johnny had said about the writings and artwork his father had produced. He said, "Leave it with me. I need to secure those writings!"

# Chapter 13
# In Memoriam

Philip announced that he and Nan had been consulting a local stone mason about a gravestone for Granddad Johnny. A date had been arranged for a little ceremony the following Monday at the graveside so that Mule could be in attendance before returning to Houston. Philip had met Mi Yong during the cross-border escape that he had coordinated and they had developed a very humorous 'banter' between each other during that time. Mule and Mi Yong invited Philip to watch them teach me. The theme for this week was 'Striking with the Legs'. We warmed up with Mi Yong's routine and then went into practising standing kicks with forward and reverse strikes using different parts of the foot for different types of kicks. We practised knee strikes for very close combat.

Philip was very interested and kept wandering around us watching even the tiniest of movements whilst not saying a word. I then had to demonstrate my arsenal of spinning kicks with the two of them breaking down the movements into their constituent parts and reassembling them for more power and greater agility. I was sweating profusely by the end of the session and although glad to finish, I felt more accomplished than I had ever been before.

Mi Yong told me that I had something that many fighters would give a great deal for. I had the ability to anticipate what a person would do before they did it. That split second would always give me an edge. Philip was very complimentary about the training as well. The two of them looked at him in a wondering way and asked if he had any proficiency in 'martial arts'. Philip said, "I wasn't too bad a boxer in my youth. When I joined the Marines, I had unarmed combat training. That was further developed in the 'navy seals'. I tend not to fight unless it's really necessary and I certainly do not see it as a leisure activity or a sport."

I responded by saying, "I presume you think it's a good idea for people to learn how to protect themselves though?"

He replied thoughtfully, "Yes, of course. It is important to learn how to defend yourself. I suppose what I'm trying to say, rather clumsily, perhaps, is that real fighting is brutal, savage and deadly. Life-or-death close combat is not a game, past-time, sport or leisure activity. I suppose my experiences have left me resenting the skill sets that have been drummed into me in a lifetime of training to kill. Nightmares exist in the minds of those who have a conscience, particularly about the bad things they have done for their country! I could not bring myself to fight anyone now unless I or someone dear to me was under threat. You can talk your way out of most situations if you display confidence!"

Mi Yong responded to this by saying, "It is much easier for a person to show that level of confidence if they know that after the talking has failed they can deal with the situation in a more confrontational way!"

We all left the garage for a cold drink with Mi Yong and Philip continuing the discussion. Mul Yong and I rolled our eyes at each other and left them to it. I had a PE exam that morning so I showered, had breakfast and headed to college.

The auction, we were told by Dad, was to take place the following Saturday. Philip looked up the name of the auction house and downloaded the catalogue. He seemed very interested! He returned to stay at the Castle House Hotel and invited Mi Yong and Mule for an evening meal there. He also went with Mi Yong to visit the cathedral again. Mi Yong had become very attached to the building and the atmosphere it created. She felt it was a spiritual place, even for people who were not religious. Philip was very impressed by the SAS stained glass window, although he felt it was a little too modern for his taste.

On the day of the auction, Dad was on a live feed to the auction house and sat through all the lots. At the end of the proceedings, the large items had been bought for:

Amphibious Vehicle—£75,000; Willy's Jeep—£17,000; Pink Panther—£78, 250 Matchless G3/L—£6,000; Royal Enfield Constellation—£12,500; Matisse Desert Racer—£12,000; Vincent Black Lightning; £825,000. A grand total of £1,025,750. Dad contacted his mum with the news. She was obviously delighted. The other items from the storage unit would come up for auction at a later time.

The next day, there was a knock at the door and a man enquired if Philip Morgan lived at the property. We obviously said that he didn't but that he did visit. Well, the man said that he had been given the address, and he had a large item to deliver so we agreed to accept it. He came back up the drive with, guess what? It was Granddad Johnny's 'Royal Enfield Constellation'. We were all very surprised. About thirty minutes later, Philip appeared at the door asking if his delivery had arrived. Dad said to Philip that if he had known Philip was so interested in the bike, his mum would have given it to him!

Anyway, Philip was so excited, and in anticipation had bought two helmets. Mi Yong and Mule came out to look at the bike and Philip handed over a helmet to Mi Yong and said, "Do you fancy coming out for a spin?" Mi Yong's face lit up with delight and she climbed on. Philip jumped on and away they went. We didn't see them again until the evening! When they did return, Mi Yong's face was a picture! It was very red from the wind and her hair was dishevelled but her eyes sparkled with joy! To say that she was invigorated by the experience would be an understatement. Philip seemed very pleased with Mi Yong's response to the day out on the bike but in a very quiet sort of way. We were all regaled with the main points of the day by a quite breathless Mi Yong. She said that she had been on a motorbike in North Korea but it was a very inferior machine compared to the bike Philip had.

Philip had explained that the 'Royal Enfield Constellation' had been Johnny's bike and that he had loved the bike and had lavished many hours on its maintenance and appearance. She had then loved the time even more. I sensed that the two of them were getting pretty close, which was a wonderful thing to see. Dad contacted Nan and told her about Philip buying the bike at the auction. She was surprised but agreed to reimburse what he had paid for the bike as she felt sure that Johnny would have wanted Philip to have the bike.

On Saturday night, Dad was contacted by the Security Services who were in somewhat of a flap. Apparently, Yi Cheongdung Yong, the Foreign Affairs Minister for North Korea, whilst on a diplomatic mission to South Korea had defected! The authorities in South Korea were afraid of the repercussions his defection would mean in their relationship with the north and had asked the British Security Services for advice on what to do. As his mother was in the UK, staying with us, the British government and therefore the Security Services had agreed with some reluctance to give him political asylum granting him protection and a country to stay in temporarily.

Whilst the knowledge he could give about the regime would be invaluable, the intention had always been for him to stay in the North Korean government and provide information about current political machinations. Kim, would not be happy about this seeming betrayal. Because of this threat, Cheongdung would need to be protected for some time. Dad was given the responsibility of organising his protection and told that Cheongdung would also be staying in Hereford with us. Life was getting complicated. With that knowledge, Mul Yong cancelled her return to Houston, as she could not miss the opportunity to meet her twin brother.

On Monday morning, we all prepared to travel to Llanelli to attend the unveiling of Granddad Johnny's memorial stone. We would travel in two cars. Mum would take Mi Yong, Mule and Philip with her; whilst I would take Rhianna and Liam. Where was Dad you ask? Well, on Sunday evening, Dad went to pick up Cheongdung from Terminal 2 at Heathrow Airport. He had been busy arranging a protection team for Cheondung and the four teams of two close protection officers with firearms would meet him at the terminal with a mini-bus for transportation. They would spend the night at an undisclosed safe house before making their way to the hillside cemetery of the Welsh Baptist Chapel near Llanelli. Cheongdung, it seems, was intent on attending the ceremony!

It was mid-May. It was a beautiful, warm, sunny day as our entourage slowly strolled up the winding path back to the final resting place of Granddad Johnny. There was not a cloud in sight; unlike that sad day back in March. The chapel gardeners had obviously been very busy as the grass had been recently mowed and 'strimmed'. Not a tuft of wayward grass worried the boundaries of any of the graves. All was neatly trimmed and not a weed to be seen. The scent of spring flowers was in the air with many of the graves having fresh flowers: mainly tulips, late-flowering daffodils and a smattering of roses. A less tantalising smell of garden waste being burned wafted over from a neighbouring garden.

Thankfully, the smoke dissipated in the light breeze before reaching our small gathering. The memorial stone had been placed in position and covered with a lovely green silk fabric with white tigers and red dragons on it. We were all positioned so that we could see what it said on the stone. Cheongdung stood next to Dad with Mi Yong and Mule on his right side. Nan stood next to Dad on his left, with Mum, me, Liam, Rhianna and Philip alongside. Uncles, aunties and cousins stood to our left. The close protection team were scattered around the cemetery; alert to any access points. They were all armed. Even Dad had a bulge on the left side of his suit jacket! There was even a military helicopter flying wide circles in the clear blue sky. Security was being taken very seriously!

Dad stepped towards the silk fabric and paused before saying, "I think I should make a little speech before unveiling this memorial stone. Johnny Morgan, my dad, was always a man of humbleness. Everything he did was understated and he did not readily take the limelight. Well, I now feel more able than ever to speak about him and perhaps for him, having gained an insight into his life through various sources. He was a remarkable and courageous man. He was also, unfortunately, a man of few words, therefore, in many ways, undermining our understanding of what sort of man he was. As a young man of seventeen, he witnessed his mother being killed by his war-traumatised father. Whilst attempting to stop his father he was badly hurt to such an extent that they feared for his life.

Nevertheless, he survived and had the mature understanding not to blame his father but to accept how a terrible wound can make a man insane. He visited his father as often as he could; he saw the anguish and despair that tormented his father over the killing of his wife and the damage he had done to his son. Bill Morgan could not forgive himself and in all honesty, his children found it even harder to forgive. His family paid an exacting price many years later for the awful injury incurred in the brutal, hand-to-hand fighting, in 'Mametz Wood' during the First World War. The events of that terrible day changed the direction of Johnny's life and certainly made his brother and sisters take a different course in their lives. He joined the army and saw action during the Second World War which prepared him for a less conventional military service.

In 1950, he went to Korea and worked with an American special operations group behind enemy lines. During that time, he met a lovely lady by the name of Mi Yong; who we are very fortunate to have with us today. They fell in love and she became pregnant. They planned to marry at the end of the conflict. Mi Yong went into labour whilst Johnny was away in Japan reporting on the successes of the partisans. The partisan stronghold was attacked and reports came back to Johnny that Mi Yong had been executed and that his daughter Mul Yong had been taken by relatives to the north. Johnny attempted to ascertain the whereabouts of Mul Yong but to no avail and spent a lifetime wondering!

On his death, Johnny directed my daughter Kerry to a diary that he had kept recording events of his life; mainly associated with his military career. It was through the diary that we found out about Mi Yong and Mul Yong. If only Dad had revealed this information! But as I've said he was a man of few words. Unfortunately, on this occasion, action did not speak louder than words!

Through my contacts and Philip's, we ascertained that the information given to Johnny was inaccurate in many vital ways. Mi Yong had not been executed at Kwanumsa Temple but taken with her father and brothers into captivity. Mul Yong had not been taken to the North with the Yi clan but had been found abandoned and given up to an orphanage near the Imjin River. Later, at the age of three, she was taken for adoption in the USA. With the assistance of the Colt adoption agency, we made contact with Mul Yong and here she is today. None of us realised that there was to be another surprise but more of that in a moment. I decided that as Mi Yong had been taken to the north then she could still be alive. There is little opportunity for the people in North Korea to have any contact with the outside world as the state forbids it.

So again, with help from contacts both Philip and I have; we explored the possibility that Mi Yong still lived. Oiling wheels within wheels gained us the information we were looking for. We intended to just talk to Mi Yong initially but had put in place a backup plan in case she was willing to escape with us. My dad would have been proud of his younger brother's organisational skills in planning a complicated extraction, particularly when the person being extracted could barely see. I spent two days with Mi Yong and during that time, Cheongdung, Mul Yong's twin visited. During the attack on the Kwanumsa Temple, Cheongdung was saved by his captured grandfather during the temple attack and they were interred in a political prisoners camp to be later joined by Mi Yong. Johnny never knew that Mi Yong had given birth to twins!

Anyway, Cheongdung, who is a very high-up official in the North Korean government, was alarmed at first by my presence. However, Mi Yong calmed him down and insisted that she would come with me to the west to meet her long-lost daughter and sort out problems with her eyesight; and, of course, here they all are. To complicate matters a little further, Cheongdung has decided to defect, thus the reason for the security presence.

Dad was married to my mam, Mildred, for fifty-four years. Mam and Dad loved each other dearly and their relationship was a partnership and a friendship. Neither would knowingly hurt the other. As you can imagine the revelations about Dad's life before he met Mam have had quite an impact on her. She has been shocked by Dad's unfathomable secrecy; nevertheless, she has accepted and welcomes Mul Yong, Cheongdung Yong and Mi Yong into her life. As do the rest of the family. After all, Mule and Cheong are Dad's children and therefore have a part to play in the lives of this family.

So today, we are gathered together to commemorate Johnny Morgan by the unveiling of a memorial stone. He would be so pleased to see all the people he loves here to commemorate his life. We have arranged for us all to go for a meal together and have also arranged for some accommodation to be provided in the event that whilst we are celebrating Dad's life a little too much falling-down juice is imbibed. Could I now ask my mum and Philip to step forward and do the honours?"

Nan and Philip stepped forward and released the green silk. The fabric fluttered briefly like a beautiful, delicate butterfly in the light breeze before coming to rest on the ground. The memorial stone was made of grey granite with gold leaf lettering. Carved along the edges were images of white tigers and in the centre was a ferocious red dragon also outlined in gold leaf, just above Granddad Johnny's name. The stone read:

*__Johnny Morgan__*
*__1925–2018__*
*__He is loved__*
*__Seek and ye shall find.__*
*__Knock and the door shall be opened.__*
*__Ask and it shall be given!__*
*__Matthew Chapter 7 verse 7.__*

As we moved away from the memorial stone what can only be described as loud continuous bangs were heard. Dad shouted, "Gunfire! Get down!" Different sounding bangs broke out on the footpath moving up from the chapel and also followed quickly by gunfire from the upper entrance where vehicles could access the cemetery site. I have never heard gunfire before but it isn't like anything you would hear as an ordinary civilian. We were surrounded immediately by the security personnel who used their bodies as shields shouting for us to get down into a large depression near Granddad Johnny's grave.

Dad drew a weapon from a shoulder holster beneath his suit jacket and so, amazingly, did Mum! She had a very nice dark blue suit on. She moved her right arm to the back of her jacket just above the waistband and pulled out a weapon. Mum and Dad with four members of the security detail took up a defensive cordon around the rest of us. No fuss. It seemed to be all in a day's work. The shooting didn't last for more than seconds. There was a short silence before people started shouting that our group were to stay where we were until things had been sorted. Minutes passed before the sound of police cars and ambulances was heard. A little while later, our group was herded down the cemetery footpath, passed the chapel and to our cars. There were two bodies of a male and female near a rather large black gravestone which had the figure of, what I can only describe as, a 'guardian angel' looking down on the deceased. I quickly glanced at the writing on the stone and it indicated that a two-year-old boy was buried there. The 'guardian angel' certainly had not protected the two assassins.

As we left the grounds of the chapel, a taped cordon was being set up by the police so we had to duck through before being told by Mum and Dad that we were going to proceed as planned and head for a meal and drinks at a local hotel. Our stunned and very quiet group went to the various cars and headed off, trailed still by the security detail; leaving the police to secure the site and deal with the inevitable uproar that would follow. Would the incident get to the national press I wondered?

When we arrived at the hotel, Mum and Dad told us all to go inside and have a deserved drink whilst they went for a debrief with the security team. This we did and about fifteen minutes later, Mum and Dad joined us. Unusually, Mum did the talking and this is what she said, "First of all, the security team thanks you for being so cooperative and making their jobs of protecting you easier by your willingness to comply with orders. Two Asian couples entered the two access points of the chapel grounds carrying bouquets of flowers. They were challenged by the security details but chose to ignore the officers. They were challenged again and told to stand still, drop the flowers, put their weapons down and put their hands up. They carried on walking. Shots were fired over their heads; at that point, the couples split up and drew their weapons.

The helicopter, which had on board two snipers, took out the couple nearest to our group whilst the other pair were neutralised by the team on the ground. We believe it was an assassination attempt on Cheongdung. We have left the local police to clear the site and go through the usual protocols pertaining to an event of this nature. Whilst I know you must all be shaken up by this turn of events, I must reassure you that all is well and you are safe. The incident will be reported to the national press but not as it really happened. There will be some bending of the truth to suit our circumstances. I cannot say anymore!"

We left the bar area and proceeded to the dining room. No one spoke. I looked at my brother and sister. They were white with fear and stared straight ahead. I didn't know how we would be able to stomach food after such a horrific event.

However, we did! A lot of alcohol was imbibed by those old enough to do so. After we had dessert, I got up and asked if I could say something. Once again everyone looked surprised!

I had found another note alongside the letter to Mul Yong that I found secreted away in the lining of the box. These are Granddad's words:

*Mildred, I love you so much! You have stuck with me all the way and you have been the most loyal loving friend and wife! I know I'm cantankerous and stubborn so thanks for putting up with me. You have every right to be angry with me for not telling you everything about my life before I met you. I just couldn't bring myself to hurt you so I took the coward's way out. Because of the work I did with Special Forces, I had to be a very secretive person and keep my own counsel. However, the secrecy should never have encroached on my family and personal life. I am so proud of our children!*

*I wish our grandchildren every success and happiness in the lives they lead and that you all will occasionally think of me! Mil, I know it will be hard to adjust to life for a while, but I know you are a strong person and that you will keep on keeping on. Please do find someone else because you deserve to be happy!*

*I know we have enough money to pay for funeral costs and I would like there to be a proper do afterwards so that everyone can have a bit of food and drink on me whilst perhaps remembering me!*

*To our children: The three of you have been a credit to your upbringing (a compliment there to good parenting)! Mum and I are so proud of what you have done so far in your lives. Never stop wanting to improve yourselves—it is so important not to give in on bettering yourself—no matter how old, you should always have something to aim for! If I had my time again, I would have wished that when you were little we would have had a little more money so that the three of you could have had a little more and that I was a little softer and less disciplining; I could also have been a more cuddling sort of person (for that I am sorry!)—but hey you didn't turn out too bad!*

*Just as a little extra surprise—you may have seen a lady in her seventies at my funeral who is rather striking in appearance. She would likely have bodyguards with her, remain incognito and show no sign of being part of any group. I'm sure, Kerry, with a little bit of thought, you can come up with an answer to that puzzle.*

At that point, I did puzzle! The woman and the two young men! Not her sons but there to watch over her, to protect her, just like the protection team surrounding us today. She was an important person! Oh, how silly of me. The lady is the same 'royal' that Granddad rescued all those years ago! Doh! I said out loud, "For those of you at Granddad's funeral, do you recall a smartly dressed lady who wore a hat with a jaunty feather and was accompanied by two very fit, well-dressed young men? Well, that was 'Rose', a member of the royal family whom Granddad rescued after she was kidnapped. Everyone looked nonplussed except Dad."

That evening, we stayed in the hotel. Philip and Dad remained in the bar swapping stories of their adventures whilst drinking too much. Mul Yong, Mil Yong, Mum and Rhianna went to the leisure pool, jacuzzi and sauna annexe. Liam went to his room and so did I. I put on the television and watched the ten o'clock news on BBC 1. A famous Llanelli boy was the presenter. This is what he reported:

*Earlier today, there were multiple shootings in the West Wales village of Llwynhendy. Reports suggest that several people were killed. The killings took place in the cemetery of the Welsh Baptist Chapel of Moriah. It is believed that the victims are of Asian background. A press release stated that the police are investigating the causes of the incident and the subsequent deaths. The area has been cordoned off and an investigation unit has been set up in the chapel. The police suspect a turf war meeting between Asian gangs went horribly wrong.*

The report came to an end so I went to find Mum to tell her what had been on the news. She was very calm and relaxed about the whole business. She went on to say that the news report would be altered in another couple of days and a more realistic closer to the truth scenario would be presented. She felt that it was a good opportunity to make the Korean contingent of our family disappear so that they could all live their lives out of the spotlight and out of danger. I said that perhaps it was all right for Cheongdung and Mil Yong to disappear but what about Mul Yong? She is an American citizen after all. The Americans take a dim view of their citizens being murdered. The ramifications could be enormous. Mum just shrugged and said, "Do you think that only Cheongdung was the target? I think their intelligence services knew about all three and this was an intended hit to wipe out their whole family."

"You mean us as well?" I stated incredulously.

"We cannot be certain about that," Mum responded. "The North Korean government's intelligence agency would have certainly found out that your dad had visited Kaesong in order to speak to Mil Yong; that he had met Cheondung, and that he had been able to take an almost blind elderly lady across what is supposed to be an impenetrable border. Let's just say that the North Koreans would be a little 'miffed' about their intelligence apparatus not being up to muster and leave it at that. I am afraid that all three of them are going to have to disappear. A sort of 'witness protection' programme for foreign nationals."

The following morning at breakfast, Nan wanted to speak. This is what she said, "I have spent a great deal of time processing what Johnny said in his black book. His conservation of what has gone on in his life before he met me has almost certainly prevented him from meeting Mil Yong, Mule and Cheondung. A little more openness would have given him all that he desired! He provided well for his family and did so even in his passing. I have decided to give our Korean family the 'gogok' pieces, twelve in all, that were given to Johnny by Mil's father as a reward for rescuing her.

These pieces will enable you all to start a new life in a comfortable manner. I had to get that off my chest as it had been playing on my mind for some time. The incident that we all witnessed yesterday and the subsequent fallout with the three of you having to begin new lives, goodness knows where has brought clarity to my thinking. Alan can advise you on the best way to sell the jadeite pieces. May you live your lives in peace!"

With that, Nan sat down and continued with her breakfast in a very subdued manner. Mil, Mule and Cheongdung all went over to her and thanked her most profusely for her generosity. She smiled and for the rest of the morning looked pleased with the decision she had made.

Mum and Dad spent a great deal of time that morning talking with Cheongdung, Mil and Mule, I suppose discussing the options that they collectively or individually had. Then they spent a lot of time on their mobiles making arrangements with the decision-makers in our government.

# Chapter 14
# Epilogue

In April 2021, Mildred Arianwen Morgan at the age of 82 died, three years after her beloved Johnny. Her health had deteriorated considerably in those intervening years. As everyone will know, the COVID-19 pandemic had the UK in its deadly grip at the time. She did not die of COVID-19. Some would say that she died of a broken heart. Her twin sisters had both developed 'dementia' with Eilwen, the 'Miss Trunchbull' type figure fading away rapidly. Whilst Eleri, the one with the diminutive frame, sadly had to go into a care home and caught the dreaded virus there.

My dad was away when Nan was admitted to the hospital. He was contacted by one of his brothers requesting that Dad return home immediately as the medical team said Nan had only a short time to live. He rushed back from an undisclosed location only to be refused admittance by the hospital staff as there was no patient visiting during the pandemic. He tried to explain that the ward she had been admitted to initially had called it 'end of life' only to be told by the nurse that they had no records of that being the case. These wards were in the same hospital and in passing a patient from one ward to another ward, no information of such importance had been exchanged.

My dad asked that her condition be verified and would they contact him immediately as he would sit in the car and wait to hear from them. He gave his number. Later, after waiting three hours in the carpark, he was phoned by a relative to say that the nurse had been trying to ring him. The hospital had got in touch with the relative about my dad not responding to the calls only to ascertain that the number taken had been written down wrongly. In the meantime, Dad drove home to Hereford in a deeply anxious state only to be woken at three in the morning by his brother stating that Nan had died peacefully in her sleep. Apparently, a night shift nurse was the last person to have spoken to Nan. The lady had said, "Good night, my lovely!" and Nan had replied, "Da boch chi. Breuddwydion melys cariad! Goodbye! Sweet dreams, love!"

As I write this, I feel like howling with indignation and outrage, but the times were strange and my dad whilst exceedingly upset also understood the difficult circumstances all NHS hospitals were facing.

Nan's funeral took place in the same place as Granddad's. At least, Nan wanted to be buried! Only 25 people were allowed to attend so only very close friends and relatives of the deceased could attend. We all had to wear face masks. There was no congregational singing but appropriate hymns were sung on a CD player that Mr Thewlis kindly supplied. Dad wanted to deliver the 'eulogy' but was not allowed to, so Mr Thewlis collated memories that we all provided. Ironically, considering the power of technology these days, Mr Thewlis did not have access to the internet or own a computer. He was a man of the pre-computer age even though, he was probably younger than my dad. In fact, come to think of it, his whole demeanour and the way he spoke seemed to be of a bygone age. A man, capable of writing a letter and using the telephone! All correspondence was by post.

Dad drew together what our little family had to say about Nan and posted a letter to him. His brothers and anyone else did the same. On the day of the funeral, we met outside Nan's house, socially distanced and 'masked' of course. It was a warm April morning with beautiful blue skies. It was the same funeral directors that had been used for Granddad's funeral although this was a much-reduced affair because of 'COVID-19 restrictions'.

Let's be honest, the pandemic was a major drama but the numerous lockdowns had sapped people's spirits and excitement was in short supply. Many of Nan's neighbours stood at a respectful distance from the ensuing spectacle. The hearse with Nan's remains appeared first. There was one wreath of flowers placed on the coffin. Nan was not a fan of flowers outside of their natural environment. She had been a keen gardener with Granddad Johnny but had never liked cut flowers. She felt they looked better on the ground. The hearse reversed into the drive and remained parked up for fifteen minutes so the neighbours could approach and pay their respects. Then three stretched 'Jaguar' limousines pulled up and as Dad was the eldest son, we climbed into the first vehicle. Dad's brothers and their families then boarded the other two but in order of age. The lead funeral director wearing a rather splendid black top hat and long black coat moved into position in front of the hearse. He turned to the hearse, bowed and lifted his head in one respectful movement before removing the hat and placing it under the crook of his arm. He turned and the hearse started to move slowly off after him.

Our limousine followed as our slow procession proceeded to head for the chapel at a slow man-walking pace. The limousine had cream leather seats with shiny walnut trim around the edges of the passenger cabin. My sister Rhianna said, "If he's going to walk all the way, it should take another thirty minutes at the pace he is going and the service is in ten minutes!" Thankfully, he climbed into the front of the passenger side of the hearse after about 400 metres and we travelled at a much more conventional speed to the chapel on the hill. Dad and his brothers and cousins were not allowed to be pallbearers because of 'covid' restrictions.

Inside the chapel, the pews were partitioned off so that there were always two metres between mourning family 'bubbles' with yellow tape blocking the seating in between. Once we were all sat down, that was the end of all movement from the congregation. The funeral service could only be 30 minutes long so the readings and hymns (sang by a CD anonymous choir) were delivered at break-neck speed and at the end the 'eulogy' was delivered by Mr Thewlis. Mr Thewlis delivered the memories that the 'family' had given him to say and even though he had known Nan as a member of the congregation for twenty-five years he said very little that could be perceived as coming from his own personal experience of 'knowing' Nan. He said something that was absolute nonsense about Nan. He talked about Nan being a keen 'international traveller'. That certainly wasn't the case.

She had taken a day trip to France once and been to Bulgaria on a week's package holiday with Granddad. She certainly could not be regarded as an international traveller. She rarely left Llanelli. It made me feel annoyed that he had so few memories of his own to say about a long-serving member of his congregation considering how few were left attending that chapel. He certainly did not seem like the 'good shepherd' who attended to his flock's spiritual and religious needs. Anyway, I must sound positively grumpy!

The service came to an end and we proceeded to make our way to the plot where Granddad was buried. Obviously, a hole had been dug in preparation for the internment of Nan's coffin and the commemorative stone had been lifted and lay forlornly to one side near a pile of newly excavated earth.

There was no one this time to dance clumsily around the hole and the sombre atmosphere surrounding the restrictions seemed to dampen the spirits beyond belief. Thankfully, neither was there an assassination attempt on the mourners as had been the case during the last time we had all been to the cemetery. The minister spoke briefly at the graveside and then the little family groups returned to the vehicles and we were taken back to the small courtyard outside Nan's house. As we were not allowed to have a 'wake', we all said our farewells and went our separate ways. Our little family group stopped at the motorway services at Penllergaer. Mum and Liam went to get some hot drinks from the Costa Coffee outlet whilst the rest of us set up the pink travelling chairs we always took with us for picnics. We ate our own sandwiches and cakes and talked about Nan and our memories of her. We laughed and cried but it wasn't the same as giving someone a proper send-off.

What became of the Korean contingent I hear you ask? Well, I cannot answer as they went into protective custody and have been placed somewhere safe.

Philip has settled near us in Herefordshire and visits us often.

I didn't become a primary school teacher. I had very good grades at 'A' level and joined the army. Specifically, the Royal Corps of Signals regiment. I'm a lieutenant. My aim is to be selected for 264 (SAS) Signal Squadron based at Sterling Lines in Hereford. Once I have established myself there, I will apply for SAS selection. I know that women have passed elements of selection but they have never been allowed to attempt the entire process. It is my intention to challenge that decision-making. So, wish me luck!

Liam left school as soon as he could and joined the Royal Electrical and Mechanical Engineers Regiment.

Rhianna is training to be a nurse. Dad still works as an 'intelligence operative' and his boss is Mum, both domestically and professionally. Apparently, she has always been his 'superior'.

I don't know if you remember me saying that when we visited the storage facility, there was another black book; in fact, there were two books. One book contains a lot of Granddad's exploits after the D-Day landings and later in Palestine. The second covers more stories about Korea, the Vietnam War and various operations he conducted after those world-important events. After a great deal of reading, I did find some information about the rescue of his brother Philip from a POW camp on the border between Vietnam and Laos.

Granddad Johnny asked me to write his story and this I have done to the best of my ability.

My experience as a writer isn't great as you've probably noticed whilst reading. However, my heart has always been enthused by the subject matter. The root of the story goes right back to the day he was sitting at breakfast with his mum, dad and two-year-old brother Philip. The terrible events of that morning influenced and shaped Granddad Johnny's decision-making for the rest of his life. I thought it would be pertinent to let his father, Bill Morgan give voice to his feelings as to what happened.

Granddad Johnny transcribed a letter that his father had written to his five children not long before he passed away.

Here it is:-

*Forgive me, my mind was not my own. I know you can't—just as I can't! My mind was in a muddy, bloody field beside a leafy, green wood. Indelibly printed memories of those days of carnage sewn into the very fabric of my soul without a glimmer of hope of ever coming back!*

*I loved your mum and I loved you all. Vivid, waking nightmares wracked my mind interspersed with cogent moments of care and security. Make your peace with God, our corporal roughly uttered! Bayonets fixed, up over the top, not ever expected back! The morning I murdered your mother and hurt you so badly, Johnny, I often attempt to recall why I committed such a heinous crime. Up into no man's land, walk don't run and keep your shape was the voiced order. Line after line of obedient khaki, never ever coming back!*

*It's as if a fragment of my memory has been removed and whilst I know I did a terrible thing, I cannot grasp the detail or the reason why. I do know I was infused with an uncontrollable anger that had me in its grasp. Wave after wave of walking Welsh. Officers with pistols at the ready. The cream of their generation. No hope of ever coming back. I will never be able to forgive myself and do not expect forgiveness from my children. I will go to hell for my crime!*

*The deadly hail of rat-tat-tat indiscriminate machine gunfire scything down a harvest of healthy young bodies strewn in deadly repose over a muddy field. I survived the carnage, wounded yes, but still I got out alive. But did I survive really? I don't think the part deep down in my soul had a chance of escape. The guilt and embarrassment for having survived whilst other better men had not. You cannot blame yourself, Johnny, for the insane actions of your father. I have always appreciated the fact that you came to see me and tried to understand what had happened to my mind.*

*I know that what you experienced that morning cannot be obliterated from your mind, the detail being too stark and violent to expunge. But I also know that you are a good person and that you will have done good things for others, perhaps to make up for the bad things that happened to you. I'm sorry and I love you all!*

## The End